# For We Are Many

ALSO BY

Stuart Thaman

---

The Goblin Wars Part One: Siege of Talonrend

Vatican Massacre

# For We Are Many

Stuart Thaman

ISBN: 0996086765

ISBN-13: 978-0-9960867-6-9

Hydra Publications
1310 Meadowridge Trail
Goshen, KY 40026

www.hydrapublications.com

Friday, October 22$^{nd}$, 1976

The waiting room at the hospital is noisy. Several televisions are mounted in the corners and they drone incessantly. It seems like people on the news always have something to talk about. All they ever do is just talk. Occasionally, a picture will flash up on the screen and some of those are interesting, but mostly all I get to see is people talking. The outfits that everyone wears are different each day, and that helps make the waiting room better. Today, the newsmen just talk about a baseball game that I wasn't allowed to go to. I like going to games, but lately the only place I ever get to go to is the hospital. The reporter keeps saying the word 'sweep' but I don't know what it means.

Yesterday, the only thing they showed on TV was a picture of some great big ship as it sank in a river. I don't really pay attention to the words the news people say, but I watch the pictures and stare at the screen so I don't have to see the other people in the waiting room.

The day before the ship wreck, I got to see a picture of an old Italian man who died. The news showed his face constantly and talked about how he might have been a mobster, but I never saw him holding a Tommy Gun in any of the pictures, so he must not have been.

Mr. Morris sits in the corner of the waiting room like always. He usually reads magazines, but not today. His brown suit wrinkles and makes noise as he constantly shifts back and forth on the plastic chair. He looks nervous, but then again, most of the people in here are perpetually nervous.

The fluorescent lights make everything look yellow, like the tiles and chairs and people are all sick. A nurse comes through the swinging double doors of the waiting room with a clipboard in her chubby hands. She has red hair tied up in a tight bun on the top of her head and a pair of thick glasses that do nothing for her frumpy figure.

"Mr. Morris!" she calls, and the old man struggles to stand up.

A younger man, probably my dad's age, helps Mr. Morris get to his feet and walks him over to the nurse. The younger one is wearing a black suit that looks expensive and at first I think he must be related to Mr. Morris, but then I remember a story he told me once about how his only wife had died a long time ago.

I'm sitting next to the double doors and Mr. Morris looks at me when he passes. He smiles to me like always and gives me a 'thumbs up,' but I shake my head. He doesn't know.

I walk over to the younger man and sit next to him in the chair that Mr. Morris was sitting in. I shift around like he did but the warm plastic seat doesn't feel uncomfortable. I look at the man's expensive suit but he ignores me and pretends to watch the news.

"Did you know Mr. Morris?" I ask him, wondering if he might be one of the old man's neighbors or friends.

"Who?" he asks, disinterested. The young man still hasn't taken his eyes from the television but I can tell he isn't paying it much attention.

"The old guy you walked over to the nurse was Mr. Morris. Did you know him?" I ask again but the man just shakes his head.

"That's too bad," I tell him. Finally, he bothers to look at me and his face shows his confusion. "You would have liked Mr. Morris. He was nice and always used to tell me stories."

The young man shakes his head again and looks me over as though I am some sort of unknown animal. "Why do you talk about him like that, kid?" he asks me quietly.

"What do you mean?" I put my hands in the air by my head as though I have no idea what he is talking about, but I understand. Adults always get nervous and upset when I know something they think I shouldn't. Playing dumb usually helps me avoid their questions.

"You talk about him in the past tense. He was just here," he says and a couple other patients look over our way so he lowers his voice even more. "If Mr. Morris is your friend, I'm sure you will get to see him again."

I grin because I don't want to scare him. My dad and the doctors always say that I scare people. They yell at me and say I should just be quiet and act like the other boys my age. According to the principal at school, I scared too many of the teachers and other students so they won't let me go back.

"Mr. Morris is leaving today to go be with his wife," I tell the man. He looks confused so I run back to my seat in the lobby before he asks more questions.

The receptionist's phone rings loudly on her white desk and another nurse walks through the double doors holding a clipboard. I slide off the chair and walk to the doors. The nurse is there for me. Her nametag says "Dorothy" and she is friendly. She pats me on the head as I walk through the doors and down the brilliantly lit hallway. The interior of the hospital shines with disinfectant and bright white paint which takes away some of the dreariness of the waiting area. Everything smells clean and stings my nostrils.

Machines beep and hum and doctors move around everywhere in a constant hurry. I always wondered, if the doctors are so busy that they need to jog down the hallways, why don't they just hire more doctors? The nurse walks behind me and puts her hand on my back.

"We are going to a different room today, sweetie," Dorothy says as she leads me down a corridor I have never seen before. She stops us before a big wooden door that has been freshly painted. The name plate next to the door is blank.

"Don't keep the good doctor waiting," she says. I turn the handle and let the heavy door swing open. The office is dimly lit and there are no windows. A small green lamp on a tiny desk is the only light source.

"You must be Fletcher," the doctor says with a sickly sweet voice. She stands and walks from behind her desk to shake my hand. The doctor is tall, taller than any woman I have ever seen. Her long blonde hair is held together in a ponytail and she wears glasses like most of the other doctors. Her glasses are smaller though, not the thick frames that remind me of soda bottles. "I'm Doctor Lissa Kendrick," she says with a smile.

I shake her hand and sit down on the low couch across from her desk. She pulls her chair around and sits across from me. With her back against her desk, the doctor's body nearly eliminates all of the soft light from the room. She crosses her legs and I notice the high-heeled leather shoes that must have made her look so tall.

"You're new here, aren't you?" I tell her more than ask. Dr.

Kendrick looks at Dorothy standing in the doorway and nods.

"You can leave now, nurse," she says curtly. "Thank you."

Dorothy smirks. She brushes the wrinkles out of her uniform and looks to me and then at the doctor. "Don't let his cuteness fool you," she says. The nurse leans in to Doctor Kendrick's shoulder and whispers, thinking I can't hear her. "Don't hesitate to call us if you need any help. He will get in your head. This little guy is strange."

I try to hide my smile, but I like when the nurses and doctors talk about me as though I'm not sitting in the room. They think that just because I am only thirteen years old, I don't understand their whispers. I take advantage of their arrogance.

Doctor Kendrick has a large manila folder that she thinks will tell her everything she needs to know about me. "So, it says here that your father brought you in a couple months ago for psychotic behavior." She puts little air quotes around the words 'psychotic behavior' and flashes her disarming smile.

"I guess so," I say quietly and stare at my shoes.

"Why don't you tell me a little about why someone would choose the word psychotic when describing your behavior?" Doctor Kendrick flips through a few pages of the file and shakes her head.

"I don't know," I say quickly. I haven't done anything. I never hurt anyone and I don't really like being in hospitals all of the time.

The sound of hurried footsteps and shouting outside the door piques Doctor Kendrick's interest so she cracks the door open just slightly enough to see the commotion. I can hear Dorothy's panicked voice among the squabble and the distinct noise of squeaky stretcher wheels flying across the tile. "What in the world?" she says under her breath.

I close my eyes in the dark room and smile. "That was Mr. Morris," I tell her calmly. "He just died during one of his cancer treatments."

Doctor Kendrick hesitates. "And why is that?" she asks, ignoring her notes for the first time.

I shake my head solemnly. "I don't know. I'm not the doctor here." I kick my feet against the bottom of the couch to show my impatience.

Doctor Kendrick scoots her chair a few inches closer to me and says with a stern tone, "How did you know that Mr. Morris was going to die?"

"I don't know. I told you, I'm not a doctor."

The therapist gets up and sets her folder of notes down on her chair before excusing herself and going into the hallway. I wait just a few seconds before reaching out and flipping the stack of documents open. I see my picture paper-clipped to the first sheet. It is a photo of me in my baseball uniform from last year that used to be framed and sitting on the nightstand in my dad's bedroom.

The door opens swiftly and Doctor Kendrick laughs. I try to flip the folder back to its original position but she has already caught me. "Thought so," she says, her voice filled with glee. "So it seems the nurse was right, Fletcher. You *are* a clever one."

"Sorry," I say, defeated. She shuts the door and returns to her post on the chair in front of her desk and looks into my eyes. With her hair pulled back so tightly, her face seems overly angular and foreign. Her eyes tilt up at the corners just slightly enough to make her radiate a certain kind of exotic beauty. In the soft light of the windowless office, her pale skin and light blue eyes are flawlessly enticing.

"Did you kill Mr. Morris?" For a moment, her voice loses its subtle, melodic gentleness and takes on a sharp edge that betrays her nervousness.

"He had cancer…" I say, but my voice trails off, struggling to overcome the sudden lump in my throat. Our eyes are locked and I want to look away or bolt out of the office but I can't.

"Did you kill Mr. Morris?"

Sunday, October 24th, 1976

I like going to Sunday school every week. It makes me feel like I'm normal again since the doctors and my dad won't let me go back to my regular school. An hour before the service starts I get dropped off at the Methodist church where my mom used to go until she died. Dad never went to church with us, but he never does much of anything except for work. All he ever wants to do is go on sales trips and drive to business meetings.

"Alright students, today's message is about Jesus performing miracles," the instructor says with a cheerful voice. Mr. Davis, the Sunday school teacher, is a fat man. He wears baggy sweaters every week to church even though the building doesn't have air conditioning and it usually gets hot inside the classrooms. That just makes him sweat and by the end of the class he smells like old cheese and beer.

There are only a handful of other students in the class because the church congregation is small and mostly comprised of older people. None of the kids sit by me. They all used to be my friends, but when I got kicked out of school, they stopped talking to me. Sometimes I hear their parents whispering about me in the hallways like Dorothy and Doctor Kendrick did. I understand everything they say and I know when they are about to tell secrets about me because of the sidelong glances they all use.

"We are going to read from the gospel of Mark today, children," Mr. Davis goes on. His great big belly heaves and jiggles with every word. He looks like a giant Christmas ornament in his bulky sweater, sitting on one of the short chairs meant for little kids. He looks around the room at all of the students, doing his usual scan to see who remembered to bring their Bible. I always have mine, but most of the other kids don't bother to bring one.

"Fletcher," he says with a genuine smile, "would you mind

reading to the class?" Before I have the chance to respond, he points to the old Bible in my lap and tells me the chapter and verse.

"'And they came over unto the other side of the sea, into the country of the Gadarenes. And when He was come out of the ship, immediately there met him out of the tombs a man with an unclean spirit'," I read aloud, taking the unfamiliar passage slowly. All of the other kids in the class groan.

"We don't like his version," they complain. "Yeah, the King James Bible sounds weird," another says, adding to the chorus of discomfort.

"Quiet down now, class," Mr. Davis says. He is always too nice. The teachers in school would have yelled at the other kids for talking over someone when they were reading aloud. Mr. Davis says that he never raises his voice because he needs to save it for singing. The loudest member of the church choir, Mr. Davis claims that he used to be an opera singer with a promising career. I don't think anyone would pay to see such a fat man sing in a dorky sweater. "Larry, why don't you pick up where Fletcher stopped," he commands as nicely as possible. Some of the kids chuckle; whenever Mr. Davis wants something done, he always has Larry do it. The arrogant kid always wears the same red sweatshirt every week to Sunday school and is always eager to impress all of us. Larry glares at me before starting to read.

"'This man lived in the tombs, and no one could bind him anymore, not even with a chain. For he had often been chained hand and foot, but he tore the chains apart and broke the irons on his feet. No one was strong enough to subdue him. Night and day among the tombs and in the hills he would cry out and cut himself with stones.'" Larry is the best reader in the class and quickly speeds through the section with ease.

Mr. Davis lifts a meaty hand into the air to stop him. "We have read about Jesus casting out demons before, right?" Everyone nods. It was a common theme in our Sunday school talks because we all found the dark subject of demons rather interesting. "This time, Mark tells us that Jesus talks to the unclean spirits." With another gesture from Mr. Davis, Larry continues reading.

"'For Jesus had said to him, "Come out of this man, you impure spirit!" Then Jesus asked him, "What is your name?" "My name is Leg… Leg-i-o-n,'" Larry sounds out the letters, unsure of how to pronounce the word.

Without thinking, I correct Larry. "Legion," I chime in. "For we are many." Mr. Davis nods and smiles before asking Larry to continue the reading. I listen to the rest of the story with mild interest as my mind wanders. After proving my reading abilities over the best kid in the class, I feel accomplished enough that I don't need to pay any attention to the rest of the story.

The remainder of the lecture is boring and Mr. Davis doesn't ask me to read again. We talk about pigs and the difference between humans and animals, but I consider all obvious. When I was younger, when my mom was still alive, we would sometimes go fishing on the Ohio River. We didn't catch much, but I asked my parents one day if it was wrong to kill the fish we caught. I knew that if we ate them, it wasn't immoral, but some of the fish we just cut up and used for bait to catch bigger fish. My mom explained it to me then as though it was a silly question: "You shouldn't kill animals unless you need to, Fletcher honey, but animals don't have souls, so killing them isn't murder."

I remember sitting along the shoreline and fishing with my family. My mom would wear the same swimsuit every day we went to the river. It was super tight but not the kind of small, revealing swimsuit I would see other moms wearing. Dad would complain that her swimsuit was too 'old fashioned,' but my mom was a competitive swimmer when she was younger and it was her favorite suit. I liked it. The red, white, and blue swimsuit is one of the only outfits I can remember her wearing.

As I walk from the smaller building that serves as the school house over to the main church, I notice my dad waiting in the parking lot in his car.

"Hey, kiddo!" he shouts to me and waves for me to go to him. I walk slowly, looking at the bright orange paint of the AMC Javelin. It has a cool stripe down the side which I like, but other than that, I hate his car. To make matters worse, all that my dad ever talks about is that stupid car. He is standing, leaning against the car door by the time I reach him.

"What's up, buckaroo?" I hate when he calls me those stupid

names. Mom never did that. "How was Sunday school?"

"It was alright," I say. I look through the windows of the Javelin and everything looks normal.

"What are you looking for, sport?" my dad says with an overly enthusiastic grin. I feel like ever since he made me see all of the doctors at the hospital, he acts really weird around me. Sometimes, I feel like he is a stranger and we have never met before.

"Nothing," I say, but I don't take my eyes from the car. "Why are you here?" He knows that church won't be over for another hour and a half. I always go to the service after Sunday school. I like to sit in the pew all the way in the back and close my eyes and pretend my mom sits next to me and holds my hand like she used to. Everyone just assumes I fall asleep.

"My meeting today got cancelled, so I thought I would get you early and we could go get some ice cream together," he says with a dorky grin that makes me cringe. "What do you say, champ?" He playfully punches me in the shoulder and I open the passenger side car door. I start to pull the seat forward to climb in the back, but a firm hand locks the seat back into place.

"We aren't going too far, you can sit in the front seat, ok?" I nod my head but don't say anything. He always does this when we go for ice cream, like he is trying too hard to make it more enjoyable. Sometimes I think he does it more for himself than for me. He spends so much time driving in his car that it must feel nice to have someone in the passenger seat to see.

We sit down outside the ice cream shop with two almond flavored sundaes and he asks me what I want to do today.

"I wanted to go to church," I tell him, more angrily than I intended. The following moments of awkward silence are nearly unbearable. We used to do stuff together all the time on Sunday afternoons, but since mom died, he never has any time. There is always a business meeting or a sales call or something that gets in the way. Occasionally he won't even bother to make up an excuse and he just leaves. On those days, he comes home smelling like horses and whiskey.

"Can we go to the park and work on baseball?" I ask, trying to ease the tension.

"Oh, not today, kiddo," he says, ruffling my hair as though that makes it better. "Dad has an important call to make tonight to a new customer, I won't have the time."

He doesn't realize it, but his fingertips have a smattering of pineapple sundae sauce still on them when he touches my hair. Now my head is sticky and smells like syrup. *Fantastic*, I think to myself. *I wish mom was still alive.*

Monday, October 25<sup>th</sup>, 1976

Doctor Kendrick is waiting for me when I climb out from the back seat of the Javelin. She taps her foot impatiently and my bulky coat slows me down. The door doesn't open far enough to allow even a kid to have easy passage from the backseat. I feel like whoever made the car never intended for human beings to make use of the area behind the two racing style chairs in the front. Clearly, the designer of the car company never sat back there himself.

"You're late," Doctor Kendrick says in a flat tone. She is wearing a knee length red dress under a long white lab coat.

"I know, I'm sorry, I was in the middle of a business call," my dad shouts through the open door. He flashes a smile and waves, starting to pull away from the curb, but Doctor Kendrick puts a hand on the car before he can leave.

"Mr. Lee, if you have a moment, I would like a word," she says through the open window with a voice of command. After a brief moment of hesitation, dad parks the car and slowly gets out and stretches. With his hand on my back we follow Doctor Kendrick into the hospital waiting area.

"Right this way," she leads him through the swinging double doors and into the first hallway. I take a seat across from a television mounted on the wall. I'm just close enough to where the doctor and my dad are standing that I can overhear them.

Doctor Kendrick lets out a long sigh. "I think it would be best if we begin to medicate Fletcher," she says softly. My heart begins to pound in my chest. I don't mind coming to the hospital to talk to doctors, but the idea of taking pills scares me.

"What sort of medication?" I hear my dad ask. Doctor Kendrick pauses and rustles some papers.

"I want to recommend that Fletcher start taking amfebutamone, a relatively new drug that works well to treat depression." Depression? At first I think I must have heard incorrectly, but what else could she have said? Why do they want to treat me for depression? The phone sitting on the receptionist's counter rings and I can't hear what is said next. Less than a minute later my dad pushes through the double doors and walks past me, shaking his head. I wonder why he doesn't tell me about the conversation. He probably suspects that I was able to hear it all. I can tell by the way that my dad looks over his shoulder as he leaves that he is attracted to Doctor Kendrick. She doesn't look like mom, but she is tall, and dad always likes tall women.

"You can come back now, Fletcher," the doctor says with a characteristic smile. I follow her into the poorly lit office and notice her new name plaque affixed to the wall. *Doctor Lissa Kendrick, Director of Experimental Psychology*. The small golden square with her name makes her seem more important and powerful. It does nothing to add to the gloomy atmosphere of the office.

She sits with her legs crossed in the chair directly in front of me and holds a blank yellow notepad instead of the thick file. After a long silence, Doctor Kendrick finally breaks eye contact and runs a hand through her silky blonde hair.

"I want you tell me about your past, Fletcher," she says. I notice a large square of chalk or some other light substance outlined on the wall, presumably for a window to be cut. The room could use some more light.

"What do you want to know?" I ask her, although I am positive she will make me talk about my mom. All the doctors always wanted to know about her and how she died and then they would ask how her death made me feel. How should it make me feel? My mom died when I was seven years old. I think most kids would feel the same way.

Doctor Kendrick smiles as though she can read my thoughts, a knowing grin that sends a shiver down my spine. "From reading the other doctor's notes, I can get a pretty good idea of the kind of person your mom was, but I want to know the kind of person *you* are, Fletcher. Why don't we start with something serious?" The way she speaks is entrancing. Her voice is subtly melodious with some hint of a foreign accent, but I don't know what it is. Her pale blue eyes search for my soul in the lamplight.

I nod my head slowly.

"Great," she leans back in her chair and dips her old fashioned pen into an ink well. "Start by telling me exactly what happened the day she died. I don't particularly care for how it made you feel, I just want the details." She looks at me and I squirm under her gaze. "Don't leave anything out."

"Alright," I say, trying to remember the day as best I can. It all happened so long ago that most of the details get blurred together and don't make any sense.

"Mom was gone the entire morning. I don't know what I was doing, but I think I was just watching cartoons or else reading. That's what I liked to do when I was little," I start. I can already feel a small lump forming in my throat. Talking about the day she died is difficult.

"And what was your father doing that day?" Doctor Kendrick asks as she writes down what I say on her notepad. She sounds interested, but I can never be sure with adults, especially doctors. Sometimes people ask me questions and when I respond, they get distracted or just don't care enough about the answer to listen.

"I remember that my dad was cutting the grass when my mom got home," Doctor Kendrick looks up from notes and interrupts me.

"Which part of the yard was he cutting?" she asks. I tell her the front yard because I could see him from the window and she records it verbatim. Doctor Kendrick asks where my mom was that morning.

"She was playing tennis at the Whitewater Golf and Tennis Club," I tell her. I know the name because she always used to buy me shirts from her tournaments and give them to me as presents.

"What kind of outfit was your mother wearing, Fletcher?" the doctor wants to know. I never really thought about that very much. My mom usually wore sports clothes so that is how I remember her.

"I think she was wearing a white and blue tennis outfit, one with a skirt. She was carrying her bag over her shoulder and bouncing a tennis ball on the walkway up to our front door." When I try to imagine how she was dressed, I can picture the whole scene more clearly in my head. I remember the way the ball sounded, rhythmically hitting the concrete over the rattle of the lawnmower.

"Did she come into the house?" Doctor Kendrick flips to a new piece of paper in her notebook and continues writing. The fountain pen makes gentle scratching sounds as she records my words.

"Mom walked in through the front door and tossed the ball to me. I caught it and our dog went wild. He loved tennis balls." I am so lost in my own memories that I barely notice Doctor Kendrick sitting down beside me on the couch. Something inside makes me think the doctor is tricking me or trying to use some psychological technique that I won't like. She has no reason to get so close.

"What kind of dog did you have? What was his name?" she asks.

"Her name was Corson. She was a beagle and loved to howl whenever anyone opened the door. I played with the tennis ball, throwing it for Corson to fetch all over the house. Mom went into her bedroom to shower since she had just played tennis and dad was still mowing the lawn. I played with Corson for a while until I accidentally threw the ball too far and it bounced out of the sliding window above the counter in the kitchen."

Doctor Kendrick writes everything. "Did Carson go outside to get the ball?" she asks.

"Her name was Corson," I correct her, "Corson with an 'O', not Carson with an 'A'." She dips her pen back into the ink to correct her spelling in her notes which I find oddly comforting. I feel like she cares about my dog, even though Corson died of old age a few years ago and she will never be able to meet her.

"I opened the back door to let Corson go out into the yard to fetch the ball, but she took off running faster than I could catch her." I have to stop a moment in my recollection to fight off tears.

"Where did Corson run to, Fletcher?" the doctor whispers. The dark room feels cold and unwelcoming. The couch is scratchy against the back of my legs and I just want to run from her office and never return.

"Corson went to the shed and started barking. She clawed at the wooden doors and even tried to bite them like the shed was dangerous and she needed to kill it." I take a few deep breaths to steady the rise and fall of my chest and a sharp sob escapes my throat.

"I didn't know what to do so I opened the door to see what was in there. We hadn't used the shed for anything other than storing the lawnmower, so it should have been empty." I can't help but cry. Doctor

Kendrick walks to her desk and takes a box of tissues from it and hands them to me. She sits in her own chair and beckons me to continue.

"Corson wouldn't go inside the shed so I opened the door all the way and looked in…" I can't do it. The memory is too painful to recall and my body is exhausted. Warm tears run down my cheeks and fall onto my clothes and the couch. I blow my nose into a tissue, but it doesn't help.

"That's alright, Fletcher," Doctor Kendrick says with her typical mirth. "You don't have to continue. You can tell me what you found in the shed next time I see you, alright?"

I'm thankful that she is willing to let me stop. My mind can't take the torture of that place much longer. I feel a hand on my shoulder comforting me so I nod to show her my appreciation, but when I look up she is already sitting behind her desk and putting her notepad away in a drawer.

Tuesday, October 26th, 1976

Lissa Kendrick paces the floor of her newly rented apartment. Yellow light reflects off of the wooden siding that lines her walls and starts to give her a headache. She lets her hair out of its ponytail and kicks her shoes off. A cold glass of white wine chills her fingertips as she moves back and forth across the thick carpet of her living room. The apartment feels foreign. Most of her belongings are still tucked away in neat boxes stacked to the ceiling.

The square kitchen table is the only piece of furniture the doctor unpacked other than a pair of cheap barstools. A ring of condensation spreads out from the wine bottle over the pale green Formica. A newspaper clipping greedily soaks up the moisture, but Lissa doesn't care. She has more copies of that particular newspaper.

An open box filled to the point of overflowing holds dozens of medical charts and patient histories in the corner of the small kitchen and one file lies open on the table. Her soft blue eyes have read the file more than once and still she could not make sense of it. There had to be some sort of hidden connection behind all of the medical data that would explain Fletcher's personality.

"Suspended from school for telling a little girl that he was sorry her father died," Lissa reads aloud to herself. "That hardly seems justifiable." She scans further down the page. "Ah, because that little girl went home and found a shotgun resting in her father's mouth and his brains painting the walls…" Doctor Kendrick throws the sheet back onto the table and picks another up from the folder.

A light flickers somewhere down the hallway but Doctor Kendrick ignores it. The apartment was all she could find close enough to the hospital and to say it was cheap would be an understatement. The sheet in her hand had clippings from a newspaper stapled to it with certain sections highlighted. She reads the document again, not believing that the tabloid sensationalism could possibly be true. "Boy from the Midwest brings down commercial airliner with his mind… Impossible," Lissa mutters. The light flickers again so she sets her wine glass down on the table and walks to the switch at the beginning of the hallway.

"Local 11-year-old boy Fletcher Lee calls into a radio show on September 8th, 1974, to warn the public about a tragic airline crash. When asked where the crash would happen, Lee told the radio host that there was too much fog on the ground to tell where the accident would happen and then the boy hung up." Doctor Kendrick flips the light switch for the hallway off and on and notices that her bedroom light is on and the door is open. She walks slowly down the hallway, engrossed in her reading.

"On September 11th of the same year, Eastern Air Lines Flight 212 from Charleston, South Carolina en route to Chicago, Illinois, went down just outside of Douglas Municipal Airport in Charlotte, North Carolina. Investigators have blamed a thick blanket of fog for the deaths of 72 passengers onboard." She reaches her bedroom door and fumbles around the corner of the wall for the light switch. With her eyes still scanning the sheet, Lissa flips the switch down to the off position and walks back to her kitchen.

She reaches a hand to her wine glass and sets the paper down amongst the other files that belong to the folder containing the records of Fletcher Lee. The doctor finishes her glass of white wine and sets it in the sink. With the medical file in hand, she sits down on the shag carpet with her back against the wall. "One day there will be a couch right here," she says to herself.

The living room is entirely devoid of furnishings. The thick carpet feels cool under her feet and makes her shiver from the chill. She pulls her legs in close and tucks them under her chin, becoming as small as possible. A box lying within arm's reach holds a set of folded blankets that the doctor has been using in lieu of a bed. She pulls a dark green blanket from the moving box and wraps it around her body.

Something on the back of her neck feels wet and slimy. Lissa rips the blanket away from her and throws it to the ground. She leans over the fabric to inspect it and sees an unusual dark stain.

A sudden sound steals the breath from her lungs and makes her fall back against the wooden paneling of the wall. Somewhere in one of the apartments next to hers, a massive machine sounds like it is powering down. As the noise gets softer and softer, the lights in her apartment grow dim. Within the span of a few seconds, the apartment is pitch black, except for one light. From the end of the hallway, Doctor Kendrick can clearly see her bedroom door, wide open and spilling bright light into the darkness.

She forgets about the blanket and runs down the hallway with her heart pounding. Lissa closes her eyes and slams the door shut. A small sliver of light makes its way out from under the door. She sits across from the door and puts her bare feet up against the wood.

"I need to stop drinking wine when I do research," she says and wipes her brow. A fine glaze of sweat comes off on the back of her hand. Doctor Kendrick can hear her own breathing and the rhythmic hammering of her pulse. A black shadow blocks out half of the light from under the door and she shrieks.

Consumed by terror, the doctor pushes with all of her strength against the door, expecting the handle to turn at any moment. As quickly as it appeared, the shadow is gone, replaced by light that does nothing to comfort her.

Hours later, close to sunrise, Doctor Lissa Kendrick wakes up on the floor of the hallway in her dark apartment.

Thursday, October 28<sup>th</sup>, 1976

A blaring alarm clock wakes me from my restless sleep. It is my dad's alarm clock, not mine. We live in a small house about a mile away from the house where mom died. I hate this house. The hallways are too narrow to feel comfortable and they are wallpapered with a dull grey floral print that looks out of place.

I slide from my bed and tiptoe to my bedroom door. My dad slaps his alarm and groans in the next room. There is a window in the hallway but it is covered by a thick curtain that blocks out the predawn glow. I hurry past without giving it another thought and flip on the lights in the kitchen. My dad will be up soon and I love the hour before he shambles from his room. I'm never tired in the morning, but something about the peacefulness of the sunrise gives me pause.

I open a window that faces east in the family room and return to the kitchen to start making coffee for my dad. He works so much that sitting with him at the breakfast table has become one of the rituals that I cherish. The hazelnut flavored coffee fills the room with a sweet, dark aroma and I drink it from the air. Enough coffee drips into the pot for two people, but I never have any. It tastes too bitter.

The orange Javelin sits in the driveway just outside the window. We don't have a garage like we did at the old house, so my dad bought a carport. A neat row of boxes lines the wall under the window.

Dad comes out from his room still rubbing the weariness from his eyes. He wears a business suit, but it isn't a fancy or expensive one like the man I saw in the hospital waiting room. He used to wear those kinds of suits, but since my mom died, he only wears shabby ones that have stains and sometimes little tears in the sleeves.

"Hey, kiddo," he says as he grabs a mug from the cupboard next to the fridge.

"My name is Fletcher," I tell him for the thousandth time. He smiles and pours his coffee.

"So, Fletcher," he says as he sits across from me at the table. "Tell me about this new doctor. What is she like?"

"What about her?" I ask. I know I have to go back to the hospital today and I'm dreading it. Doctor Kendrick is going to make me finish the story about the day my mom died.

"Do you like her?" He noisily sips the hot coffee with a thoughtful expression on his face.

"She seems nice. I liked Doctor Hayes too. He was always nice to me." My last doctor was an old, wrinkled man far beyond the age of retirement. His heavy glasses would slowly slide down his nose when he talked so he was constantly pushing them back up. "Doctor Kendrick is new to the hospital. She didn't even have a name plate next to her office the first time I met her."

Dad looks lost in his cup of coffee. Steam rises up from the mug and swirls around his face, bathing the room in warm hazelnut. "She wanted me to consent to have you medicated, Fletcher." I want to tell him that I know, but something inside tells me that I shouldn't. I always like to keep some secrets to myself when dealing with doctors.

A long silence passes between us. "If you want me to, I will request another doctor for you." What he says surprises me. When he met Doctor Kendrick, he seemed to like her, or was at least physically attracted to her. He never said anything like that about Doctor Hayes.

"No, that's alright," I tell him honestly. "I just don't want them to force me to take any medicine. Can you tell them no?" I try to look as sincere as possible and it seems to work. My dad's expression is one of sorrow. His eyes never leave the black surface of the coffee.

"I told her that you are against medication, for now." He looks defeated. "Fletcher, I know that things haven't been the same since mom died. I understand that. My business has been slow, I haven't made a sale in a few weeks, and things are tough for us." For a moment it looks like he might cry. He sips his coffee instead. "I need you to step it up with this doctor, buddy. If she really wants to, I think she can force you to take medication."

He stands and finishes his coffee. With his back to me as he places the mug in the sink, he laughs under his breath. "I want to see you back in school after the Christmas break, ok?" His jovial tone betrays the doubt in his voice. I know what he thinks; I will never go back to school. Too many people are afraid of me.

Dad picks up one of the boxes from the row and ruffles my hair before saying goodbye. Keys jingle in his pocket as he walks outside and unlocks the Javelin. I run to the window and watch as he loads the box of dental equipment into the truck. The sun is cresting just over the gently sloping roof of our neighbor's house and casting eerie shadows into the crisp layer of morning fog.

Something dark falls out of his pocket as he slams the trunk lid closed. I tap on the glass to get his attention, but he just smiles at me and waves. I point down on the ground by his feet and he still doesn't understand. I'm not sure what he dropped, but something certainly fell from his left pocket. Moving quickly, I flip the lock on the top of the window and slide it up so he can hear me.

"You dropped something!" I yell to him. He looks down at his feet, searching the ground by his right shoe. I see it. A small, jet black streak of shadow is lying on the concrete. The shadow is out of place. Silently, the shadow moves. A quick glance confirms that no birds or other animals are nearby to cast the shadow.

Dad bends down to look closer, but he is checking the wrong area. The shadow lengthens and becomes thin, almost rigid, like a black, incorporeal arrow. The thing moves forward, toward the open window. I can sense the shadow's awareness. I want to scream but fear has a solid grip on my lungs that it is unwilling to relinquish.

"Dad," I manage to whisper, but he can't hear me. He stands and opens his door with a shrug. As he steps into the driver's seat, the shadow follows. It races up the orange paint and wraps itself around the metal frame. I try to point again but my white knuckles won't budge from the windowsill. A fingernail on my left hand cracks and trickles blood.

Something is sitting in the back seat of the Javelin. The engine roars to life and the car rolls backward. Dad turns his head, looking at the road as he backs away. How can he not see it? A pale, naked arm stretches out and catches the sharp line of dark shadow.

It looks like a man is sitting in the center of the car's back seat. My throat constricts and pools of tears form in my eyes that make everything look blurry. I blink them away and focus on the man. He has long hair, stringy and unkempt. He wears no clothes and his body lacks all discernible human features. His poise and the way he sits with his broad shoulders is masculine.

The creature's head turns, just slightly, and it watches me. There are no eyes set into the white flesh. No mouth, no nose, just skin. It sags and hangs loosely from the featureless face.

The car is in the road and my dad waves, just like every morning. I feel a warm line of urine begin to soak my shorts and legs. Whatever is in the backseat of that car, my dad can't see it. The wrinkled head cocks slightly to the side, like Corson used to do when she wanted a treat. I gasp for air. The javelin jolts forward as the transmission engages and the featureless being evaporates into mist. I stand in the window, frozen by terror, and look directly into the dawning sun. It is the only place left where I can look and see no darkness.

Friday, October 29th, 1976

"Hello?" A strained voice crackles through static on the telephone. "Hello?" The man sounds old and haggard.

"Yes, is this Doctor Hayes?" Lissa asks into the harvest gold receiver. Her fingers mindlessly play with the spiraled cord, twisting and stretching it as she moves about the kitchen. A cold glass of water sits on her kitchen table.

"Who is this? Murphy?" The retired doctor asks. His thin voice borders on senile.

"Doctor Hayes, hello, this is Doctor Lissa Kendrick, from Middletown Regional Hospital?" She speaks slowly and enunciates each word as best she can. There is a short pause in the static and she can hear voices in the background of the other line.

"I don't know any Kendrick. What do you want? An old man doesn't have all the time in the world, you know." A fit of sputtering coughs accents his words.

"Doctor Hayes," she says loudly, almost yelling. "I am the new psychologist currently treating Fletcher Lee. Do you recognize that name?"

Another static filled pause makes Lissa's hand flex around the cord. Her frustration continues to mount with each second of delay.

When the doctor's voice returns to the line it is steady and calm, sounding twenty or thirty years younger. "Oh dear," he says softly. The phone shakes in Doctor Kendrick's grip. "Are you at home currently, doctor?" he asks.

She lets go of the phone cord and turns anxious circles around her green kitchen table. "Yes, in my apartment, I just moved in. Why?"

"I'll be right over. Don't leave." More voices clutter the line and Doctor Hayes coughs into the receiver once before it clicks.

A sharp knock on her door jolts the doctor upright. Her glass of water flies from her fingers and lands with a dull thud on the carpet. "One moment," she calls out. Once the glass is in the sink she walks to the door and slowly turns the handle, not sure what Doctor Hayes looks like. It was an hour since she called him and Lissa had fallen asleep at the table.

"My, you're a pretty lass," Doctor Hayes says when the door opens. Giving no thought to decency, the old man looks her over and grins to show his approval.

"How did you know where I live?" she asks as they both sit down at the table. Fletcher's medical records are scattered over a pile of newspaper clippings.

"I'm old," he says, flashing what few teeth remain in his wrinkled mouth, "but not quite dead. I still have many friends in that hospital." A surprisingly firm handshake steals the doubts from Doctor Kendrick's mind.

"So," she says, unsure of where to begin. "What do I need to know about Fletcher?"

The old man doesn't respond but instead pores over the documents scattered on the table. Some papers he tosses aside without a second glance and others he pauses to inspect. After a few moments he lets out a profound sigh and looks Doctor Kendrick in the eyes with a gaze made of steel.

"You only have the very beginning of Fletcher Lee's history in this file. Where are all of my notes? My journal? His family history?" The man is visibly upset and shuffles the papers, looking from one to the next with concern. "Is this all that they gave you?"

Doctor Kendrick nods. "Yes, that's everything I was given when they brought me on to council Fletcher. How much am I missing?"

"Let's start from the beginning," Hayes says with a grim look. He coughs and pounds his chest to clear his throat. "April 30th, 1963, the day Fletcher Lee was born to Rich and Melinda Lee. Does that date mean anything to you, doctor?"

She thinks for a moment and shakes her head. "I don't know."

"Aside from being exactly 18 years to the day after Adolph Hitler killed himself," Hayes begins, "it is an ancient pagan holiday. Walpurgisnacht, or sometimes referred to as the Night of the Witches, is a somewhat important holiday in German and northern European folklore. It is said that every year on April 30th, witches from all over the world gather on the highest mountains and make great fires to commune with spirits." Another bout of coughing sets him back in his chair for a long while.

"Now, aside from this bizarre pagan ritual, you must understand a certain folksy obsession with mountain shadows." A confused look crosses Doctor Kendrick's face. "There is an optical illusion called a Brocken Spectre that occurs when someone standing on a high mountaintop with the sun at their back looks out to a thick cloud bank. When the light is blocked by the person and their shadow appears on the droplets of fog, the shadow is often much larger and usually quite alien in appearance."

Lissa holds up a hand to interrupt the story. "What does this have to do with Fletcher Lee? Was he born on a mountaintop during one of these pagan rituals?"

"No, no," Hayes says with a chuckle, "of course not. As I was saying, the shadow that the viewer casts of themselves is incredibly large and distorted by the elevation and the water droplets of the mist. If you watch the Brocken Spectre long enough, you can even see it move. The refraction of the light by the water can make the shadow appear alive and sentient, a most frightening sight indeed. Now, on Walpurgisnacht, the night when witches go to the mountaintops to play with fire, you can imagine how they view the Brocken Spectres."

"I still don't see how this has anything to do with Fletcher, but I'm listening." Doctor Kendrick tries not to be rude but she can't help but think that the old man has gone off on a pointless tangent.

"Alright, more to the point then. As it turns out, Fletcher Lee was not scheduled to be born on April 30th. He was born after only 32 weeks in the womb, a full two months premature. Melinda Lee went into labor around dusk and gave birth to a healthy baby boy an hour later."

"Eight weeks early," Doctor Kendrick shakes her head in disbelief. "He should have died. How much did he weigh?"

"That's the thing," Hayes chuckles, "he weighed almost nine pounds and was completely formed! Since the doctors anticipated a still born or at least an emergency birth, the family requested that a priest be present at the time of birth. Once the doctors determined that little

Fletcher was seemingly unharmed by his early departure from the womb, they handed the child over to the priest for baptism."

Lissa Kendrick is horrified. "I can see where this is going now," she mouths silently to herself.

"As the story goes, the priest on call that night didn't even work for the hospital where the baby was delivered. He took the newborn Fletcher and then vanished. The police were called in and the parents went mad looking for him. When they finally found the boy two hours later, he was soaking wet and crying on the rooftop of the hospital." Doctor Hayes leans over the table as he speaks, deadly serious.

"My God…" Lissa swallows hard and tried to imagine what it must have been like for Fletcher to be kidnapped moments after his birth. "His parents must have torn the building apart…"

"Since the fake priest who stole the child was never seen again, it can only be presumed what his motives were. The witches and Wiccan believers who celebrate April 30th as Walpurgisnacht will tell you that on that specific night, the shadows have power. They say that shadows are actually openings into the realms of darkness and that great spirits use the Brocken Spectres to travel across planes of existence." Doctor Hayes leans back in his chair and rubs his hands over his weary eyes.

"I was on staff at the hospital when it all happened. That night was one of the most horrifying moments of my life. People reported seeing strange shadows cast in rooms and hallways where the lights were on. A record number of patients died that night due to the rapid onset of various illnesses and one young woman lost her life on the operating table during a simple appendectomy. One moment, the procedure was going fine. The surgeon said that a sinister looking shadow appeared on the wall of the operating room and the girl on the table vomited so much of her own blood that she died before they could start a transfusion."

A heavy tension grows between the two psychologists. Doctor Hayes can hardly believe what he is saying and Doctor Kendrick doesn't want to believe it.

"So, moments after his birth, Fletcher Lee was involved in some sort of crazy pagan shadow ritual on the one night of the year dedicated to witches." Her hands tremble as she speaks.

"Now tell me, doctor, have you noticed anything strange since you first met Fletcher Lee?" Hayes smiles. He knows the answer just by watching Doctor Kendrick react to the question. "I suggest that you get a cat. They can sense the shadows better than we can. Many pagan cultures believe that cats actually ward off evil spirits."

"I think I will, thank you, Doctor Hayes." Lissa Kendrick looks down at the scattered documents covering the table. "I like cats."

Sunday, October 31st, 1976

Sunday mornings are always awkward at my house. I like to go to church but I wish my dad would go along with me. "I have too much work to do, Fletch," he says. Or he will make some sort of excuse about an important business call he needs to be home for. I know why he really doesn't go though. Dad is afraid that going to church will make him miss mom too much and he will cry. One of his friends took him out to dinner for his birthday once and accidentally made reservations at the same restaurant that mom and dad had their first date. He didn't even make it through the doors before breaking down in tears. Anything that reminds him of mom needs to be avoided.

"Are you going to Sunday school today, champ?" He sips his steaming cup of hot hazelnut coffee and reads the newspaper. I nod my head. The sun has risen over the line of houses and pours in through the window at my back.

"Today is Halloween. I bet Mr. Davis is going to give an interesting lecture on ghosts and demons today," he smiles. Dad knows that I like reading about that sort of thing but he doesn't know exactly why. He and my mom never showed any interest in spiritual beings.

"I know," I respond. "Can I get a new Bible?" I ask him, holding up my leather bound King James. The book is well worn and the cover is soft from use.

"What's wrong with Grandpa's Bible?" He takes the book out of my hands and casually flips through the pages. "You always liked this Bible. Do you use it much in class?"

"Yeah, of course we use it." I take it back from him and cling to it, suddenly worried that I might lose it. "I just... I don't know. The other kids don't like how the old words sound and they make fun of me."

He shakes his head, clearly annoyed. "Who made fun of you for having a King James Bible? Mr. Davis didn't say anything about it, did he?" I shake my head and try to wave it off but dad asks again.

"This kid named Larry who always wears a red sweatshirt every week. He said that my translation sounds funny and laughed at it. I don't like reading aloud with Larry there." I stand up from the kitchen table and walk over to the window.

Dad comes over and kneels beside me. He isn't very tall compared to other adults and he likes to kneel when he says things that I need to take seriously. I'm about an inch taller than him and it feels strange. I wish he wouldn't do that.

"If this kid Larry gives you any more trouble, you just tell him that your Bible has been in our family for years and years. It is the same one that my dad took overseas in World War Two. And besides, it can't be that different, can it?" He doesn't understand what it's like when they laugh at me during class. I shrug my shoulders and walk to the door.

"Alright," he says behind me, resigned and saddened. "Let's get you to Sunday school."

I check the car thoroughly before I dare to even touch the orange metal. That thing has been lurking around the Javelin from the day my dad bought it. I know that something is wrong, but if I tell anyone, they will drug me and lock me away forever. It is bad enough that I'm not allowed to go back to school for a while. "Can I sit in the front seat today, dad?" I ask, hoping to never go into the back again.

He hesitates before answering. I take his pause as a no and slide the chair forward so I can crawl into the back. "Oh, I guess so. We aren't driving more than 2 minutes anyways. Hop in, kiddo." I slam the seat back and jump in, glad to not be near the naked shadow man who sits in the back.

The short drive to church is uneventful. We stop at a red light momentarily and I think that something brushes against the back of my neck but it must be the wind. The window is down and the chilly autumn air feels good.

Mr. Davis welcomes me to the class as I walk through the door but Larry scowls. "Alright class," the overweight teacher begins, "last week we learned about Jesus casting demons out of a crazy man who lived in the tombs. This week we are going to talk a bit about

Halloween. Is everyone going trick-or-treating?" The class lights up like Mr. Davis just announced a free ice cream event.

All of the kids talk about what kind of costumes they are going to make. Larry is going as a homeless man, but I think the idea is stupid. Everyone is talking so loudly that it takes Mr. Davis a few minutes just to quiet them down.

"Does anyone know what Halloween means from a religious perspective?" He asks once the class settles down. No one responds, not even Larry. I'm not sure I know, but I have an idea so I raise my hand.

Mr. Davis points to me and I can see Larry scowl from the corner of my vision. "I've never been out trick-or-treating, but we always celebrated October 31$^{st}$ as Reformation Sunday." I always feel like I'm the odd one out who never does anything right.

"Well, Reformation Day is a little different, but the Halloween tradition as we know it comes from the holiday of All Hallows Eve, or All Saints Day." It's clear from the blank expressions around the room that everyone just associates Halloween with free candy.

"All Saints Day is when Christians around the world gather to celebrate and honor the saints," Mr. Davis says with a smile. "We are supposed to pray for the souls of all of the believers that have gone before us and ask God to protect their souls."

Larry asks a question. It makes me smile to see that he doesn't automatically know the answer to every question. "Where are their souls?" he wants to know.

"That's a good question, Larry." Mr. Davis usually says that when he answers a question he feels we should already know. "The souls of the saints are up in heaven with the Lord, Larry. That's where the souls of all believers go when our bodies die." I know all of this but it gets me thinking.

I raise my hand. "Where did the souls of the demons go when Jesus ordered them to leave the man at the tombs?"

"Well Fletcher, the demons were cast out of the man and into a herd of pigs that was living on the hillside, like the reading tells us." Mr. Davis flips his Bible open to last week's passage.

"I know, I remember that. But the pigs were drowned, right?" Mr. Davis nods as he rereads the section. "Where did the demons go after all of the pigs died?"

"Actually," Mr. Davis thumbs through the pages and scans them for answers. "I don't think that it says…" He keeps reading and a few of the other students open their Bibles to the passage and look as well. Larry doesn't. He sits on his section of couch and appears bored.

"Where did the demons go?" I ask again. I try to keep the nervousness out of my voice but I can tell that at least Mr. Davis knows that I'm unsettled.

"I would assume that the demons returned to where they come from, Fletcher. It doesn't tell us that Jesus destroyed the demons, so they must still exist, somewhere." He seems agitated and even a little upset.

"Did they return to hell?" I wonder, hoping that a multitude of demons were never allowed to live on earth and do as they please.

No one can come up with any reasonable answer.

Tuesday, November 2$^{nd}$, 1976

"How are you doing today, Fletcher?" Doctor Kendrick asks from her position in the center of the swinging double doors. Nurse Dorothy stands next to one of the hinges and uses her body weight to hold it open.

I stand up from the green waiting room chair and walk over to her. My dad is inside the waiting room with me. He never does that. I don't know why, but today feels different. He walks in front of me and puts a hand on Doctor Kendrick's back. She pulls away quickly and turns.

"Yes, Mr. Lee? Can I help you with something?" Her voice is calm and melodic but her body language suggests that she does not like to be touched. My dad takes a hesitant step back but puts on a friendly smile that looks forced.

"Um…" he stammers, averting eye contact. "I was just wondering if you made a decision concerning medication for Fletcher." He is obviously lying. My dad was going to say something entirely different but was caught off guard by her behavior.

Doctor Kendrick looks at me and sighs. "I would rather not discuss Fletcher's medical treatments with him present," she says curtly. Dad awkwardly leaves us standing in the hallway without another word.

We walk into her office and I sit down on the soft cloth couch. The room is better lit than before with the addition of a second desk lamp. "So," Doctor Kendrick begins. "Can we pick up right where we left off in our last session?"

I know what she wants me to tell her, but the memory is painful. "If you want me to," I say.

"You told me about playing with Corson. You threw a ball out of the house and she chased it. Can you start there, Fletcher?" She has her notepad sitting on her lap and dips her fountain pen into the ink well to begin writing.

"Well, when I let Corson out of the house to get the tennis ball, she ran straight to the shed." I fight as hard as I can to keep the lump from climbing into my throat.

"What did you find when you opened the door to the shed?" She whispers, leaning in close.

"I opened the door to the shed and found my mom...." My voice trails off and a line of tears warms my cheeks. "She was hanging from the wooden beams in the shed with a rope around her neck." Doctor Kendrick stops writing. She takes the manila folder from her desk and roots through the crinkling pages.

"It says in your file that Melinda Lee committed suicide, but the medical report doesn't say much else." She quickly scans another page before replacing it in the file. "What else did you see? What did your mother use to hang herself?"

"I didn't say that she hung herself," I correct her curtly. "I told you that I opened the door and she was hanging from the rafters." I wipe a stream of tears from my eyes and refuse her offered tissues.

"There was a rough looking hempen rope tied around her neck."

"What else was there, Fletcher? Tell me everything." Doctor Fletcher continues writing as I gather my composure.

"A burlap sack was tied around her head. I couldn't see her face but I knew it was her. It was my mom." Doctor Kendrick was visibly shaken by the story.

"I can't imagine how that must have made you feel," she says softly. At least she doesn't ask how I feel like everyone else does.

I wipe my eyes on my sleeve and choke back a sob. Doctor Kendrick doesn't ask me any other questions about my mom.

*****

Soft green lights display the time. Doctor Kendrick holds her phone tightly in her hand. She has been trying to call Hayes for hours and it is well past midnight. The phone line crackles and the old psychologist's voice finally breaks through the static.

"Yes?" Doctor Hayes says. He sounds out of breath and exhausted.

"Doctor Hayes, this is Doctor Kendrick..." she can feel the

tension in the line. The older man is worried and his sporadic coughing and wheezing shows it.

"Did you know the circumstances surrounding the death of Melinda Lee?" Doctor Kendrick asks in a rushed tone.

"It was a suicide, so I am told. The police report said she hung herself in a shed."

Lissa rested her forehead against the doorframe. Nothing made sense. "I know what the police report says. What do you believe, Doctor Hayes?"

A long pause follows. Something loud shakes the phone connection, like a box of heavy books falling from a high shelf. "Hello? Doctor Hayes? What happened?" A light rain begins outside her apartment and spatters the kitchen window. High altitude heat lightning dances between the dark clouds.

More coughing from the old man worries Lissa and she paces the floor. "Yes, yes, I'm still here. It will take more than a little lightning and thunder to kill me just yet. What the police report—." His voice breaks off suddenly and gives way to static.

"Doctor Hayes!" Lissa screams into the receiver. She waits for what feels like hours.

"I thought. . .I thought I saw something. It's nothing. What I was. . .What I was saying, Doctor Kendrick, is that none of the details of the crime scene are in accordance with a suicide." Hayes gulps noisily and his pace quickens. "Two things strike me as peculiar. There was no chair or ladder found in the shed and the bag placed over the woman's head makes no sense." Sounds of crashing appliances come through the line behind a blanket of static.

"What's happening, Hayes?" Doctor Kendrick's heart pounds in her chest. "Tell me what's going on!"

"A shadow, I was spooked. . .Honestly, it was nothing." His strained voice is hard to hear. The rain outside the window hastens and a resounding crack of thunder shakes the glass.

"Maybe Melinda didn't want her son or husband to see her expression so she put a hood over her face? By all accounts she was a first class athlete, she could have easily jumped to the rafters, right?"

"You sound like the police chief and medical examiner, Doctor Kendrick." The old man manages a chuckle.

"I can see how things don't add up, Hayes. What do you think happened? Who did it?" Lissa's feet create a small trench in the shag carpet as she nervously paces the floor.

"I don't—." More crashing sounds fill the receiver. Doctor Kendrick hears a muffled cry through the static and the rain. "It might have been the priest. . ." His voice is filled with pain and barely audible. "The shadows, Kendrick, the shadows. . ."

"Hayes!" she shrieks. The line is dead. Not even static fills the connection. Crying, Doctor Kendrick slowly returns the receiver to the phone base. It clicks into the wall mounted base and a sharp crackle of forked lightning erupts outside the small apartment sending Doctor Kendrick into the air with fright.

The young doctor sprints to the safety of her bedroom. Blankets are strewn about the room and a solitary mattress sits in the center. Lissa scoops the quilts up in her arms and buries herself in them on the lonely bed. The thunder, lightning, and shadows allow her no sanctuary.

Thursday, November 4th, 1976

"What can you tell me about shadows, Fletcher?" Doctor Kendrick asks me. The room is dark, illuminated by only one lamp like it was during our first session. A freshly cut window is set into the wall of the office, but a thick black curtain prevents any natural light from entering the room.

I'm not sure what she is talking about; she can't possibly see what I see. No one sees those things. I stare at her, trying to read her expression for some sort of hint.

She sighs. "Do you think your mother killed herself? Do you think she climbed up the rafters of the shed and hung herself?" Her tone is edgy, almost violent. She twitches in her chair behind her desk instead of resting in front of it and close to me. Her shiny blonde hair hangs down around her face, not her customary ponytail.

I'm not sure what to do. The featureless man sits on the couch next to me and shakes as if he is cold. His body is naked and hairless, like a blank sheet of skin pulled over a rigid skeleton. His eyeless face turns, pulling the skin of his neck tight and making it crackle. I try not to look at him, but I can tell by Doctor Kendrick's sudden apprehension that she noticed.

"Is someone sitting next to you on the couch?" She stares at the spot next to my legs and pushes her chair another inch from the desk. The lamp casts an eerie glow on the sharp features of her face.

"I… No, I don't know what's going on." I stare at my feet. Without a mouth, the featureless man never speaks to me, but I can feel his animosity whenever he looks at me. He doesn't want me to talk about him.

Doctor Kendrick stands. "Fletcher, if there is something in this room with us right now, I need you to tell me." I lift my gaze just enough to see her face and shake my head. She looks around the room frantically, searching the darkest corners for any signs of movement. "What is happening, Fletcher?" Her voice is full of fear. The humanoid pile of skin and bones arches his back as though he is laughing. I can tell that he enjoys fear. "Why do you keep looking to your right?" she screams at me. "What is it?"

I choke down a forceful sob and try to tell her what I see. "Sha. . .Doctor. . ." Her eyes bore into me and I know that she is both terrified and full of rage. "The shadows!" I manage to yell at her through a face of snotty tears.

Doctor Kendrick hits the light switch on the wall so hard that the plastic cover cracks. The lamp on her desk is still dark. I bring my legs up onto the couch and hide behind my knees. I clamp my hands over my eyes and wish for everything to end. I can see my mom's lifeless body hanging from the rafters of our shed in the shadows of my mind. The featureless man stands behind her. He laughs and waves his pale arms to draw the shadows into his body. It isn't my memory; it is something else altogether.

Knocking over her desk in the process, Doctor Kendrick rips the heavy curtain from the window, but no daylight streams forth. She shrieks and screams, pounding her fists into the solid red brick that fills the space where glass should be.

Nurse Dorothy hurries down the hallway and pulls open the heavy office door. Fluorescent light from the hospital floods the office and Doctor Kendrick's falling fist rebounds off of a pane of glass. Both of her office lamps are shining brightly. I glance at the nurse breathing heavily in the doorway. She looks scared and confused, but the featureless man is gone from the couch.

"Is everything alright, Doctor Kendrick?" The nurse shouts into the office. "I heard an awful sound like cockroaches screeching. It was deafening, even in the hallway."

Doctor Kendrick sucks in breath like a woman about to drown. "I… I don't know what happened. Thank you, nurse. You can leave us now." She waves Dorothy away and collapses into her chair. "Nurse?" she calls to the departing woman. Dorothy turns. "Leave the door cracked open please, if you would."

Dorothy smiles and leaves the office with the door cracked. I help Doctor Kendrick right her desk and collect the files scattered around the room.

"What was that?" she asks once the office is put back together and light is filling every corner of the room.

"Sometimes. . ." I don't know how much to tell her. "I see certain things."

Doctor Kendrick finds her pen and dips it in the ink to continue her notes. "What sorts of things do you see?"

"Strange things. Shortly after my mom died, my dad moved us to a smaller house and sold most of her possessions. We sold the car she drove and my dad got his dream car, the orange Javelin. I told him not to get it, but he fell in love with the car."

Doctor Kendrick writes down everything I say. "What was bad about the car? I've seen it, the Javelin looks fine. Do you think he bought the car as sort of a replacement for your mom?" I haven't thought about that before. The idea frightens me and makes me sad.

"I don't know," I tell her honestly. "Maybe. I know that my mom never let him get a flashy sports car when she was alive. I think he just did it because he was finally allowed to."

"You said something about the car, that you didn't want him to get it. You told him not to buy it. Why, Fletcher? Why tell him not to if you knew it would make your dad happy?"

I look around the room and the bright light coming in from the window eliminates all of the shadows. I feel safe. "He took me along to trade our old car. It was a station wagon and I liked it a lot. My mom drove it. He sold the car to the dealership and got the Javelin with the man in the back seat." As soon as I tell Doctor Kendrick about the man, I can feel his presence. He isn't in the room with us, but he is somewhere in the hospital. I sense him walking around on the floor above the office.

"What man? Who was in the back seat?" She wants to know.

"The man I see. He has no face." That sets her back in her chair. Doctor Kendrick pulls a sheet from the manila folder on her desk and reads it briefly.

"Doctor Hayes recorded that you started seeing an invisible friend shortly after your dad bought the Javelin. Can you tell me about this friend of yours?" She asks with her usual charismatic flair. I can tell by her tone that she doesn't understand. Doctor Kendrick shudders.

The featureless man is on the floor right above her head. I know it.

"He isn't invisible. I see him all the time." I don't want to keep talking about him because something bad will happen. I'm not sure how to change the subject.

"Your friend is a man? What is his name? What does he look like?" She smiles again, clearly oblivious to the fear in my voice.

"He isn't my friend!" I shout at her. Why does she not understand? "He lives in the shadows and corners of my vision where I can just barely see." I close my eyes tightly. I don't want the man to come back.

"Alright." She is starting to understand. "He doesn't have anything; no eyes, no mouth, no nose. All he is made of is skin and bones. The shadows do whatever he wants." I talk without opening my eyes. His presence is still near but there is too much light in the room for him to be able to get in.

"What does he want from you? Why does he visit you?" I thought she understood but she doesn't.

"I don't know! I don't want to talk about him. If I could make him go away, I would," I say defiantly. I open my eyes and look at the door. I just want to leave.

Doctor Kendrick finally understands that I am finished talking about the featureless man. She has me fill out a mindlessly simple personality test for the remainder of our session while she reads papers at her desk. I've taken plenty of psychological questionnaires for other doctors in the past and this one is nothing new.

The doctor finally tells me that I am allowed to leave and she walks me out of the lobby to meet my dad. "That is quite a nice looking car, Mr. Lee," she says when he pulls up at the curb. My dad keeps the engine running but gets out and leans over the top of the Javelin.

"You like it, Doctor?" He says with a smile. I have seen him use the car to attract women before, but I have never seen women attracted to him *because* of the orange Javelin. After what I told Doctor Kendrick about the man I see in the back seat, I am amazed that she would even get near it. Maybe she doesn't believe the things I tell her.

"I do!" She says with a grin. It all seems fake; staged. Doctor Kendrick is playing my dad and trying to get something from him, but I don't know what, so I stand next to the car door and watch as it happens.

"Want me to take you for a spin sometime?" My dad says. I can't be sure, but it looks like he winks to my doctor. I wish he would remember mom. She might be dead, but he is still married to her, in my eyes at least.

"Oh, not today," Doctor Kendrick responds. A slight feeling of relief makes me sigh and open the passenger side door. I check quickly and see that the featureless man isn't waiting for me in the back seat.

"Some other time then, ok?" My dad casually replies. He motions for me to climb into the backseat. "Get in the back, buddy," he whispers. "I don't want to look like an unfit parent to your doctor."

"Say, I was wondering," Doctor Kendrick banters, "where did you get the car? I was thinking about going and test driving a Javelin myself." She runs a finger along the orange paint and lets her blonde hair fall over her face to hide her eyes.

"Yeah!" My dad says. He sounds overly excited. "If you go to the AMC dealership downtown and ask for Ronnie, he can get you the best deal. He sold me this beauty and I'm sure if you tell him that you know me, he will cut you a deal. It's the best car you will ever own." He pulls a pair of sunglasses from his light blue leisure suit and slides them onto his face as dramatically as he can. I can only grimace and shake my head.

We pull away from the hospital and I look back at Doctor Kendrick. She stands on the curb and takes a small notepad out of her white lab coat and scribbles down a few lines.

My dad pumps his fist in the air above the gear shifter and reaches back for a high-five. I slap his hand out of disappointment rather than excitement, but he can't tell the difference.

*****

Lissa Kendrick speeds out of the hospital parking lot in a 1972 Buick Skylark. The transmission hesitates and gears grind for a split second as she shifts, but it is a familiar feeling. She has driven the car almost every day for the last four years and knows how it runs. She keeps the driver's side window rolled down and the wind plays through her hair like the fingers of a god. The paint is custom; a deep burgundy red that reflects the sun as a distant wildfire is reflected off of clouds hovering at the horizon. She hugs every turn and speeds through the city streets and into downtown.

The AMC dealership isn't hard to find. Doctor Kendrick parks her Skylark near the back of the lot and slowly peruses the rows of cars as she makes her way to the dealership showroom. It is getting late in the afternoon, but car places are always open well into the night. She lingers around a sky blue Javelin until a salesman spots and her approaches.

"Like the Javelin, do you?" He yells far too loudly for their close proximity. She nods and turns, trying to look disinterested. As she suspected, the salesman doesn't let her go so easily. "The Javelin sure is a fine automobile. The best sports car on the market today!" He gives the roof of the car a hearty pat to accentuate his statement.

"It looks impressive," Lissa says, "but do you have one in black?" She pretends to know nothing and the salesman takes her bait.

"Right this way, ma'am." He guides her a couple of rows closer to the showroom and proudly stands in front of a black Javelin that has an impressive white racing stripe down the center. "What makes you choose the Javelin? It sure is a lot of car and can be overwhelming for a woman to drive." The pudgy salesman wears a tie that is either tied far too tightly or else is a clip-on. His checker printed suit is clearly made for a man with a less rotund stature and his imposing belly threatens to shatter his belt buckle every time he turns or gestures.

Lissa pulls her white lab coat around her shoulders, feigning a chill, just to remind the salesman that she is a doctor and likely an easy sale. "I just moved to the city," she says innocently, "I need a new car and a friend told me to come here and look at the Javelin."

A greedy smiles breaks out on the salesman's round face. He licks his lips excitedly and begins to show all of the various features that the black AMC Javelin has to offer.

"My friend," Doctor Kendrick whispers, drawing the salesman in, "he told me that I should only deal with a salesman named Ronnie if I want the best price." The tall blonde woman hesitates just a moment, watching the overweight man think. "Does Ronnie happen to be working tonight?"

He scratches his head and looks back at the showroom. "No, Ronnie doesn't work here anymore." The salesman shudders and puts both of his hands in his pockets. "Ronnie died from a heart attack a few years ago, I knew him well. He was a good guy."

"I'm so sorry," Lissa says with a hand on the man's big shoulder. She sizes him up and figures that she would be taller than the salesman even without her high heels.

"Yeah, well, any deal that Ronnie would give you, I can give you. You don't have to worry." Doctor Kendrick smirks at the salesman's overt greed and attention to his possible sale.

"Actually. . ." she waits until the man steps closer to her before continuing. "I was wondering if you might be able to look up some information concerning the deal that Ronnie gave to my friend." The salesman looks confused and suspicious. Doctor Kendrick knows she has to make something up quickly or she will lose him. "You know, he always brags about the price he got, and I want to be able to tell him that I got the best deal this dealership has ever made." He nods his pudgy head and takes a step back, considering the proposal. "I really want to buy a black Javelin," Lissa adds bluntly to help her ploy along.

The salesman's confusion melts into a sly grin and Doctor Kendrick can't keep from giggling with pleasure. "I'll wait here and sit in the car and see how I like the interior. Do you think you can get me the sales records for an orange Javelin sold to Rich Lee sometime around the fall or winter of 1970?" She is half-tempted to kiss the salesman on the cheek, but can tell that she has him fully ensnared.

Half an hour later, the poorly dressed salesman hurriedly walks back to the black Javelin and startles the doctor awake. Embarrassed for having fallen asleep in the driver's seat of the car, she quickly composes herself and gets out. The man hands her a small stack of papers and she smiles. "Thank you," Lissa says as she closes the car door. "I am going to take a look at these tonight. I'll be back tomorrow and we can sign the papers on this sale." She adds just enough of a subtle laugh to her tone to make the man squirm under the weight of her beauty.

"I'll be looking for you then, ma'am." The salesman's balding scalp starts to sweat from the excitement of a potential sale. Lissa stretches a hand out and it is eagerly met by a firm and clammy shake.

"What is your name?" Doctor Kendrick asks him. "So I know who to request tomorrow in case you are with another customer?"

Lissa Kendrick returns to her car with a few pages of sales records in her hand. She didn't bother to pay attention when the salesman gave his name and she hardly remembers a word that he said the entire evening. The drive from downtown to her new apartment is thrilling enough in her deep red Skylark, but Doctor Kendrick's happiness quickly dissolves. She hates the sickening knot of fear in her stomach every time she turns the key in the lock. All of the lights in the apartment were left on when she drove to work in the morning and she breathes a sigh of relief when she sees that they are still on upon her return.

"I need to stop at the pound tomorrow," she mutters to herself. "I still don't have a cat."

Saturday, November 6th, 1976

Lissa Kendrick walks briskly down the aisle between the pews at Saint Timothy's Episcopal Church. The building is quiet and dark. The strong mid-day light makes the beautiful stained glass that adorns the end of each pew come alive. Colors reflect off the polished wood and polished brass candelabras. Doctor Kendrick pays little attention to anything except the black door behind the altar. A vivid crucifix watches her silently from the rafters.

"Come in, come in," the holy man beckons as he opens the black door. Lissa shakes his hand and walks into the pastor's office.

"This place is almost as bare as my apartment," she remarks. The walls have no paintings and only one dusty window offers light. A simple wooden desk sits in the center of the room and piles of old books are stacked in the corners.

"The needs of a pastor are simple, doctor." Pastor Santiago wears a black robe tied about his waist with a length of rope. He is a slight man, frail and thin in his old age. His rumbling voice reminds Lissa of Doctor Hayes.

"Yes, I see that," she jests. "I am thankful that you were able to meet with me on such short notice." She takes a seat in the only available chair and crosses her legs.

"Anything I can do to help a wayward sheep in my flock, I will." His smile is warm and inviting. Doctor Kendrick can't place the smell, but a strange aroma of cedar and dark chocolate tickles her nostrils.

"Of course," she says as she takes an overflowing file from her leather briefcase. "How familiar are you with Fletcher and Rich Lee?" She hands the pastor a photograph which he immediately gives back to her.

"I know them well, doctor. No need for pictures." He rubs his bald head and wipes a bead of sweat from his scalp. The church is not air conditioned and the small room is stuffy and hot. "Fletcher Lee is somewhat of a troubled child, I'm afraid."

"Yes, well, I am a psychologist. Everyone I see in my profession is called 'troubled' at some point or another in their lives. What makes you say that Fletcher is one of those kids?"

"He attends Sunday school regularly and is in church for almost every service. His mother, Melinda, she was the spiritual rock of the family. Since she passed, Rich almost never attends services and I have barely spoken to him." Pastor Santiago stares at Lissa with a serious expression.

"How well did you know Melinda Lee? What can you tell me about her death and how the family coped?" She has a notepad sitting on her lap and has to remind herself that she is not conducting a session of therapy.

"Melinda was a big star in college sports. She won money for the family by fencing and playing tennis. When she would travel for a televised tournament, she would always tell me which churches she found to attend on her trips." The old pastor smiles and leans back in his chair.

"When she died, it tore the whole community apart." Pastor Santiago hangs his head and sighs. "The official story that the police told to the media was that she killed herself. One of her best friends was a victim at Kent State so they believed that she hung herself out of grief, but none of us believed it."

"I'm sorry, Pastor, but if you could be a little clearer… Exactly which part did you not believe?" Doctor Kendrick asks.

"That she killed herself, of course," he says with a chuckle that holds no joy.

"And why do you think that?"

"Melinda Lee was never the type. I can tell you that with certainty." Pastor Santiago clasps his hands over his chest and breathes deeply. "I worked for a long time as a counselor for inner city youth and single mothers. I helped them cope with the hardships of life and some of them, despite my best efforts, couldn't handle it. Those were the ones who ended up in prison or in the ground. I could usually tell within the first hour of meeting someone from the inner city if they had it in them to commit suicide. It takes a unique kind of person to even contemplate something like that. They have to harbor thoughts of death for years until it consumes them. You can tell."

"Yes," Doctor Kendrick says softly, "I know what you are talking about. I have only lost one patient in my history as a doctor to suicide, but I know the look. Something evil grows within them until death is the only thing they think about and the only door that appears open. Of course, some people are experts at hiding their grief from the world and then in one moment of profound sorrow, they are capable of anything."

"Melinda wasn't like that. She was full of life. Melinda Lee loved coming to church and was always surrounded by friends, definitely not the type of outcast who would even consider suicide for a moment." Pastor Santiago pauses so Lissa can write everything he says. A bird lands on the window sill and pecks idly at the glass and its shadow hovers on the table for an instant before the creature departs.

Doctor Kendrick prompts him with a quick look. "The people who hide everything deep inside and then kill themselves, those are the ones you find clutching a tear-stained suicide note in one hand and an empty bottle of pills or a smoking pistol in the other," the robed man continues. "Melinda Lee was found with a burlap sack over her face and a thick cord of hemp tied around her neck. She loved little Fletcher," he says with authority. "Why would she put him through all of that?" Pastor Santiago works himself into a sweat.

"Look, I'm not saying that she did it!" she exclaims louder than she intended. For some reason that she cannot place, her nerves are starting to fray. "I just want to be absolutely sure that people close to her think she was murdered before I even entertain the thought. Now, was anything going on in her life that might have set off a trigger?"

Pastor Santiago dabs the moisture from his forehead. A long silence passes between them. "I don't know," he finally says. "Her husband, Rich, he is kind of a strange man. A little shy, I guess. He sells dental equipment for a living and according to the rumors that fly around church, he hasn't sold enough to make any real money. Most of the men will tell you that he talks and cares more about his car than his own kid."

"I've noticed his obsession," Doctor Kendrick says with contempt. "So, if Melinda Lee didn't hang herself in the shed behind her house, who did? Someone had to put her there. Even if she was killed somewhere else, there has to be a reason for her body to have been found in the shed. The burlap sack over her head makes me think it was suicide and she just didn't want people to see her expression, but then why wouldn't she kill herself on one of her tennis trips?"

"That's a fine question," Pastor Santiago responds. He sets a wrinkled hand down on the cover of a heavily worn Bible. "Only the Lord knows that now."

Doctor Kendrick ponders for a moment, thinking back to what she learned from Fletcher's previous psychologist. "Pastor, do you believe in… how do I say this… spiritual beings?" Pastor Santiago takes another deep breath and pushes the Bible across the table.

"You can find all sorts of spiritual beings in that book, Doctor Kendrick. Most of the people who ask me that question want to know about angels and demons. What I tell them is always the same: I have not seen the physical manifestation of either an angel or a demon, but if God says that He created them and that they are among us, that is what I believe."

Lissa stops writing and puts her pen back into her briefcase. "Do you mind explaining that, Pastor? It has been a few years since I have stepped foot in a church and frankly, I don't believe in ghosts."

"I don't believe in ghosts either, Doctor Kendrick," he snaps back as though insulted. "Angels and demons are souls created by the Lord to do His bidding. Ghosts are monsters in stories that knock over lamps and send chills through children's spines to scare them into eating all of their vegetables."

"I'm sorry, I did not mean to offend you," Lissa quickly says. "I'm just curious about some things. Fletcher tells me about certain things that he. . .sees. He believes that some sort of man without a face follows him around and sits in the back of Rich's car. Please, anything you can do to help, I don't know much about angels and demons."

Pastor Santiago takes a long look at the doctor before choosing his words. "You have probably heard Christian stories about angels visiting Mary and telling her the good news, and I imagine that you have also heard Christian stories about Jesus ordering demons out of men to heal them."

Doctor Kendrick nods. "I always thought that casting out

demons was the only way someone in biblical times would be able to describe healing without much scientific advancement."

"That is the most common theory, especially among doctors." Pastor Santiago turns around in his chair and searches through a musty stack of books before selecting one and setting it in front of the doctor. "Take a look at this," he says, pointing to the cover.

Lissa touches the soft binding and moves her fingers to open it. "I said look at it, not open it!" Pastor Santiago shouts. He slaps her hand away and scoots the book a little closer to his edge of the desk. "Most people won't even touch a book bound in human skin, but you want to dive right into the bloody thing," he mutters under his breath.

"What?" Doctor Kendrick shrieks. "You have a book made out of human skin?" She grabs her briefcase and stands, sending the chair sliding along the wooden floor with a screech.

"Calm down, calm down," he says with amusement. "It is perfectly legal to own, I assure you." Doctor Kendrick remains motionless. "And besides, I was only kidding!" A toothy grin breaks out on the pastor's face and he howls with laughter.

Lissa shakes her head and hesitantly sits back down at the desk. "Do you know why I stopped going to church?" she asks. "Pastor's like you creep me out."

"Oh, it was only a joke to lighten the mood," he justifies, feigning offense. "Now, the original *Keys of Solomon* was certainly bound in human skin, but this is merely a replica. The real one is locked away in the library of rare books at some Ivy League university. No doubt the professors have probably tried to use its power to garner more donations." Another body shaking laugh rattles through the frail man's body.

"Power? What do you mean?" Doctor Kendrick asks in an even tone. She stares at the cover of the book, hesitant to touch it. The bird returns to peck at the glass window again and startles her so badly that she nearly falls from her seat. The spectacle reignites Pastor Santiago's laughter and makes him choke.

"*The Keys of Solomon*," he finally manages to say once he regains his composure. "It is a book with no known author that outlines the hierarchy of demons in Hell." He casually flips through the pages. "Don't worry yourself, doctor. None of the demons are trapped inside," he says with a sly grin and a wink.

"So, if a demon or some other spiritual entity is bothering Fletcher," she stops, unable to believe what she is saying. "I will find the demon in this book? Is it that easy?"

"Well, not quite." Pastor Santiago responds as he hands Lissa the book. She traces her fingertips over the pentagram etched into the cover. "Treat this book more like an encyclopedia of the damned. It describes demons and some of their behaviors, but it does not go far beyond that. Not many people actually believe that *The Keys of Solomon* has any truth at all, so take everything you read with a grain of salt."

"Thank you," she says, offering a hand across the table. "Do you believe in what the book says?"

Pastor Santiago shakes her hand vigorously. "I believe everything I read in the Bible, doctor. What other people write, I can't be the judge of their integrity. I thank God every day for giving me such ignorance. I suppose that if I knew all of the devil's secrets, I would have been just another suicide case you read about in the newspaper from the inner city."

"Again, I cannot thank you enough for your time, Pastor." The old man walks Lissa out of the church and waves to her as she drives away.

Doctor Kendrick balances *The Keys of Solomon* in one hand with her apartment keys in the other and two cat carriers under her arms as she enters her kitchen. The cats, the two largest and meanest looking calicos she could find at the pound, scratch and claw wildly at their plastic cages. She tosses the book on her green kitchen table and drops the cat carries onto the shag carpet.

"Alright cats, listen up," she commands them. "If there are any demons in this apartment, or any that try to get in, you two need to chase them out." She slips a treat through the bars of their cages. "Keep the demons away from me, got it?" Willow, the larger of the mangy calicos, hisses and bites the metal wiring. Evermore, the smaller cat, digs her claws into the plastic walls of the carrier. Both of the feline creatures ignore the psychologist.

"I'm not sure what I expected. . ." Lissa murmurs. She slides back the latches on both of the cages simultaneously and the cats explode into motion. Doctor Kendrick doesn't own much furniture in her newly rented apartment, but the cats seem to vanish behind anything they can find. "Wonderful," she says to the empty room. "This better work."

Monday, November 8th, 1976

I sit on the concrete step leading into the house and watch the morning traffic. The Javelin is gone from the driveway and dad has already driven off to meet with someone about business. A school bus rumbles by down the street and I see some of the kids pointing at me. It was my school bus. Larry sits near the back in his red sweatshirt and laughs at me. I wish that they could understand what was happening. If they could only see what I see, they wouldn't laugh.

Mr. Johnson walks out of the house next to mine in a light blue bath rope. He sips a cup of coffee in his right hand and waves to me after he stuffs a newspaper into the pocket of his robe. The middle-aged man takes a long draw on his cigarette and blows a cloud of smoke into the morning air. His slippers scrape against the pavement as he approaches.

"How are you this morning, Fletcher?" At least he doesn't call me by some stupid nickname like my dad always does.

"It's bright," I tell him. Both of our houses face the east and the morning sun makes me squint painfully.

"Why aren't you in school, young man?" he wants to know. Adults usually ask that question when they see me on a school day.

"I'm sick," I tell him. "I can't go in today until the doctor says I'm better." Doctor Hayes told me to say that to people who asked questions. He said it wouldn't be good to tell them about my mom's suicide and my therapy.

Mr. Johnson takes an exaggerated step backward and puts his hands in the air as if warding off a blow. "Don't breathe on me then, Fletcher!" he jokes with a smile. Another long gout of smoke shoots from his mouth to mingle with the crisp morning air. I notice something unusual about the smoke. I stand up and look away from my neighbor; I don't want to see anything in the shadows, but I know that something is there.

"What's the matter?" Mr. Johnson asks. He takes a final draw on his cigarette and stamps it out with his slipper. "I didn't upset you, did I?" I shake my head and turn for the house. "Oh, come on now, Fletcher, I was only kidding!"

"I know. . ." I stammer. "It isn't that... I should get back inside." I reach for the door handle and see Mr. Johnson in the reflection from the glass set into the front door. The smoke from his cigarette hangs in the air like a dark and stormy curtain. I glance over my shoulder for an instant to see what is happening.

A black hand reaches through the smoke and touches Mr. Johnson's balding forehead. One spindly appendage extends from the hand like a spider's leg and draws the number six on the man's skin in blood.

"Oh alright," is all Mr. Johnson says. He waves to me again and heads back to his own driveway and his own house.

"Mr. Johnson!" I call after him. I need to warn him but I don't know how. No one ever believes me. The man turns and waits for me to speak.

"You have something on your forehead," I tell him. "A smudge, or something. . ." He rubs the back of his hand against his head and looks at me. The bloody number is still there, etched into his skin. None of the blood comes off on his hand and I know that I am the only one who can see it.

"Yeah, you got it," I say. With one last kind-hearted wave, Mr. Johnson walks back into his house next door.

I don't know what the six means, but I have figured out the general idea behind numbers. Sometimes the numbers stand for days, sometimes they are just minutes. The featureless man draws them most of the time, but if there aren't enough shadows for him to form, he just sends a black hand that drips acrid slime. The fingers of the disembodied hand are like the legs of a giant spider, covered in hair and ending in sharp points.

All of the other people that the featureless man writes on end up dying. The number on their forehead is some sort of timer on their life. The first time I saw one of the bloody numbers, it was a three. My dad and I were visiting one of my uncles. Everyone called him 'Uncle

Darwin' because he was much older and sported a thick white beard reminiscent of the famous Charles Darwin. I never even learned his real name.

Uncle Darwin lived in a nursing home in Pennsylvania. According to my dad, Uncle Darwin was his half-brother and he spent his whole life working in a coal mine. He only lived in the nursing home because he lost both of his legs during a cave in and he couldn't take proper care of himself. We didn't visit him often but when we did, I always felt sorry for him. No one should have to live like he did for all those years.

As we were leaving the nursing home after our last visit, the featureless man walked out from behind a bookshelf, thin as a piece of paper. He was much weaker then, I think, because his body back then was never made of skin. A black silhouette would appear on walls or behind objects and he would send the hand out to mark people. A bloody three was carved into Uncle Darwin's forehead. There was a message on our answering machine when we got back to Ohio. According to the time of death reported by the doctor, Uncle Darwin's heart stopped beating exactly three hours after we left.

I push images of Uncle Darwin out of my head. I don't like to think about the people I have met who have died, but sometimes, I can't help it. I sit down on the couch in the living room and close my eyes. I wish I could sleep after my dad leaves to try and sell for his business, but I can't. The sun shines brightly through the windows and I dare not close the blinds. Every time I see a shadow, it makes me panic and my heart races.

I decide to walk next door and sit with Mr. Johnson while he reads a newspaper. I used to do that after I got home from school. I knock on the screen door at the front of the Johnson's house. His wife answers the door and ruffles my hair as I walk into the kitchen. "He's out back on the porch, honey," she says with a sweet voice. She hands me a freshly baked chocolate chip cookie and pats me on the back. The cookie is warm and the chocolate melts all over my fingers as I eat it.

"Thanks, Mrs. Johnson," I say through bites of the cookie. Sometimes, I think that if my mom were still alive, she would be just like Mrs. Johnson. The older woman has a noticeable air about her that feels inviting and reminds me of what a whole family should be. I bound down the carpeted yellow hallway and pull open the door of the screened-in porch, basking in the emotional warmth of the house and for a moment, I can forget about the things I see.

The feeling fades too quickly. Since the porch is on the back of the Johnson's house, the sun hasn't quite illuminated the room and cool shadows cover the table and chairs. The featureless man sits in one of the chairs across from Mr. Johnson. "Hey there, Fletcher!" the old man's face lights up with a smile.

I slide into one of the wicker chairs and try to will the shadows away. Mr. Johnson moves his newspaper and I can see the bloody number six still carved into his forehead. "What's on your mind today, little man?" He asks behind his paper.

"Just bored," I tell him with a shrug. "What are you reading, Mr. Johnson?" I try to take my mind off of the shadows and ignore the faceless man as much as possible.

The pale body of skin and bones moves. The blank head stares in my direction and it extends a spindly appendage to the center of the circular table. I try to steady my breathing but Mr. Johnson can sense my fear.

"What's going on, Fletcher?" He sets down the newspaper and folds his hands on the top of the table, inches from the spidery fingers of the demon. The skin where the creature's mouth should be tightens and I can feel him grinning.

"I… Nothing. I'm just a little tired this morning," I lie. Mr. Johnson leans closer over the table and takes a deep breath. He pushes an ashtray out of the way as he looks at me, searching for answers.

The featureless man slides a slender finger over the table and leaves behind a trail of thick, black sludge. The black and red hairs of the spider leg he has for a finger stand on end. The demon draws letters in the sludge that smoke and smell of burning leaves. I can read the syllable "de" in the strange substance and the featureless man stops. His hairy finger caresses his chin and he cocks his head slightly to the side as if he is pondering.

"Fletcher. . ." Mr. Johnson gulps and licks his lips. I can tell that he is nervous, but he can't see the featureless man. "Does your father. . ." I barely pay attention to him. As much as I try, I can't take my eyes from the demon's acrid drawing. Mr. Johnson musters his courage and speaks. "Does your dad ever hit you, Fletcher?"

I can't take my eyes from the table. The letters "profu" are spelled out clearly in a second line of sludge. The smell of the black smoke makes my eyes water and Mr. Johnson thinks I am crying. The old man gasps and slides his chair out from the table.

"I'll kill that bastard!" He shouts. I shake my head, trying to correct his assumption, but he isn't paying attention to me anymore. "Where does he hit you, son?" Mr. Johnson demands.

"No," I manage to say without looking up. The demon draws a letter "n" and then a "d", slowly making the second word of the phrase.

Mr. Johnson's bathrobe flutters as he rushes to my chair and the demon's chest heaves as though he laughs. "Come now, Fletcher, tell me where he hits you," The man says quietly, trying to be comforting. He follows my gaze to the table but he can't see the words or the smoke. An "i" is scrawled next to the "d" and the monster continues.

I can hear Mrs. Johnson yelling at us from the kitchen but her voice is steady; she is only telling her husband to calm down. Mr. Johnson grabs me by the shoulders and forces me to look at him. He breathes heavily and I have to jerk my head to avoid specks of his spittle that fly from his mouth. "Tell me where he hits you, Fletcher!"

I stand up from the wicker chair, ready to run, and steal one last glance back the table. The featureless man is still facing me, watching everything that I do. "De profundis," I slowly sound out, pronouncing the words inscribed in sludge.

Mr. Johnson shakes me again and I stare at him, anger seething behind my eyes. "No one hits me!" I scream into his face. "There is someone sitting in the chair drawing words on your table in tar and you yell at *me!*" I can't handle his accusations anymore. I point at the featureless man who laughs harder, stretching the pale flesh over his jagged bones with every soundless bellow. Mr. Johnson lets go of my shoulders and whirls on the table, knocking over the chair that the demon was seated in.

Faster than my mind can comprehend, the featureless man is sitting in the chair that is in front of the newspaper. He points a spidery finger at me and tilts his head down with anger. I can feel his animosity washing the room in hatred. "What are you talking about, Fletcher?" Mr. Johnson asks, calming down.

I let my rage boil over and smash a fist into the tabletop. Glass explodes around my hand and Mr. Johnson shrieks. Darkness blacker than the deepest night forms inside the aluminum circle that held the glass and the strange words. A spider's leg wraps around my wrist and the featureless man pulls me closer. I yell and claw at my arm but the grip is like iron. Mr. Johnson begins to wail uncontrollably and I can feel his wife's arms wrap around my chest. She tries to calm me down but all I can think about is getting the spider's leg away from my wrist.

The demon tugs again and glass crunches between my shoes and the wooden deck. Suddenly, the intense noise of the room stops and I hear nothing. The featureless man pulls me into the swirling darkness and I cannot hear or feel.

Cold air rushes around my body and I feel like I am falling, but gravity is irrelevant. With a kick of my shivering legs, I am able to turn my body over and all I can see is darkness.

A whisper like the slither of a thousand snakes invades my mind. "Welcome to the Valley of Hinnom, Fletcher Lee," it says. I try to scream and realize that my body is not breathing. No air passes through my lungs or escapes my mouth. "Welcome to Gehenna, Fletcher Lee." The hissing voice reverberates within my skull and echoes, growing louder and louder. It is all I can hear and it takes over my thoughts.

The wind accelerates and frost forms around my lips and nose. I curl my body tightly against the cold but it doesn't help. My skin is ice and though it moves, it is hard to the touch.

"Welcome, Fletcher Lee, to the mouth of Moloch, where children go to die." I cover my frozen ears with my hands but the voice is deep inside my consciousness, booming and cackling.

I collide hard with something I assume to be ground. The impact spins my vision and makes my gut churn until I heave and vomit. There is dust all around me that clouds the air and makes it difficult to breathe. I can feel my lungs functioning and the ice slowly melting from my skin.

A pain unlike anything I have ever known shoots through my back and forces me back to the dirt. The whip cracks so closely to my head that I can feel the wind. The sound is deafening. Another stroke of the whip tears a swath of blood down my spine and for the first time since I left the porch of the Johnson house, I realize that I am naked.

"Fletcher Lee," the whisper of a thousand snakes washes over me. I can tell that whoever is speaking is standing directly over me. I curl my body as tightly as I can. My breathing comes in sharp sobs that pull more dirt and dust into my lungs than air. "Fletcher Lee," the hissing voice says again so loudly that it hurts my head.

"Yes," I cry into to the dirt. I try to think of something better, anything, but my mind is consumed by pain and fear and cold.

"Welcome home."

Tuesday, November 9<sup>th</sup>, 1976

Doctor Kendrick awakens to the purring of a hideous calico cat just before her alarm sounds. She pets the animal gently on the head and tries to remember its name. "Who are you, kitty?" she whispers. The cat licks her hand and scampers off down the hallway. The tall woman showers, dresses, and sits down at her kitchen table with a toasted bagel.

One of the calico cats slithers between her legs and purrs, looking for affection. Lissa reaches a hand underneath the table and scratches the cat between the ears. Fletcher's file sits open to Rich's bill of sale from the AMC dealership. "The orange Javelin arrived on the lot just a single day before Rich Lee showed up to buy it. He paid cash…" she scans the sheet and turns it over. "The salesman's last name is never mentioned…" Lissa finishes her bagel and scoops the papers up into her briefcase.

She opens two cans of cat food and places them in opposite corners of her apartment, waiting for the calicos to appear. She can hear them scurrying around the various boxes and odd pieces of furniture that are scattered throughout the room and the hallway beyond, but she cannot see them. "Oh well," she sighs. "Come and get it, Willow and Evermore." Lissa shakes her head. "Those are silly names. Not that cats even need names; they never come when you call them."

*****

Doctor Kendrick is buttoning her white lab coat when Nurse Dorothy meets her in the hospital parking lot. "Doctor Kendrick!" she calls out frantically. "I tried to call you, there's been an accident." The frumpy, overweight woman is out of breath from her determined hustle out of the lobby.

"What kind of accident?" Lissa says hurriedly. She grabs her briefcase from the passenger's seat of the burgundy Skylark and sprints for the door. "Who is it?" she yells as she shoulders past the wide nurse.

"No, not there," Dorothy exclaims with her hands held awkwardly up in the air.

Doctor Kendrick stops her dash and turns, fixing the nurse with a confused stare. "What do you mean?"

"Fletcher Lee," she pants. The nurse bends over her knees to facilitate her breathing. "The cops were called to his neighbor's house. They found the neighbor man dead on his porch and by all accounts, the boy was the last one to see him alive."

Doctor Kendrick's heart skips a beat in her chest and her briefcase slides from her loose fingers. "What? Where is Fletcher? What has happened to him?" She can't believe the news. Lissa shakes her head and sits down on the low curb in front of the glass doors that lead into the hospital. "Fletcher wouldn't do that… He isn't a killer."

"I know," the nurse whispers. "I've known that boy for years now and he would never harm a fly."

"Where is Fletcher now?" she asks again, forcefully upset. The violent determination in Lissa's eyes make the nurse take a hesitant step back.

"I don't know. They couldn't find him at the scene. Mrs. Johnson, the neighbor's wife, is here at the hospital." The nurse tries to put a comforting hand on Doctor Kendrick's shoulder but the agitated woman brushes it away and stands.

"Is she in emergency? Was she hurt as well?"

"Closer to our section of the hospital, I'm afraid," The heavy nurse says without emotion. She brushes the wrinkles from her uniform and begins to walk back into the building. "Downstairs in one of the padded rooms, last I heard. The police took her straight jacket off, but the woman is barely moving. She just keeps muttering her story, over and over. It sounds like something that you are better equipped to handle than anyone else in the hospital."

"Yes," Doctor Kendrick says. "This should be interesting." She walks into the waiting room of the psychiatric ward and approaches the nurse's station.

"Buzz me in, please," Doctor Kendrick says. A sharp buzzing

sound behind a heavy steel door and a series of clicks lets the doctor know that it is unlocked. She pushes the door open and descends the two flights of stairs into the bowels of the hospital. Padded rooms line the narrow corridor on either side. The bright fluorescent lighting is harsh and makes Doctor Kendrick shield her eyes until they adjust to the new environment. Nurses bustle around the solitary rooms with trays of food and medicine. A pair of burly police officers sit in metal chairs outside of one room reading newspapers. The hospital rents some of their isolation rooms to the local correctional facility when they run out of space.

Doctor Kendrick flags down a young male orderly dressed in white. "Which room is Mrs. Johnson's?" she asks him. The man takes her to a small cell and signals to the end of the hallway for a nurse to unlock the room.

"Come in with me," Doctor Kendrick says to the man and he readily obeys. Mrs. Johnson sits in the corner of the room and gently rocks back and forth with her knees tucked under her chin. The woman is a mess. Her streaky black and grey hair falls over her shoulders in clumps and tangled knots. She wears a plain blue smock that fits her body loosely and ties around at several points along her sides.

Not daring to approach her, Doctor Kendrick sits down against the soft wall across from the orderly. "Mrs. Johnson?" Doctor Kendrick says. The nervous patient turns her head slightly at the sound of her name.

"Mrs. Johnson, I'm here to help," Lissa tells her quietly. "Why don't you tell me about what happened?"

The bedraggled woman crosses her legs and stares at the space between the doctor and the orderly. "There was so much blood," she groans.

"Where was the blood?" Doctor Kendrick asks. She scoots closer to the unstable patient and tries to soothe her. "I don't work for the police. You can tell me everything. I only want to help."

"Blood," she mutters almost incomprehensibly.

"Tell me about the blood, Mrs. Johnson. Was Fletcher there? Was Fletcher Lee in the room?" Mrs. Johnson's eyes flash with anger at the mention of Fletcher.

"That devil!" she suddenly roars, clawing the padded floor. The orderly rushes to her side and grabs her arms, pinning them down. "Get off of me!" the woman howls. Her body shakes uncontrollably with a series of violent tremors and spasms.

"Let her go," Doctor Kendrick tells the strong orderly. He looks at her for a brief moment before releasing Mrs. Johnson and retreating to the door. It takes almost ten minutes for the older woman to calm down enough to speak. She tears two of the fingernails from her left hand with her thrashing but shows no signs of pain.

"Mrs. Johnson," Doctor Kendrick speaks to her with a stern voice of authority. "Tell me what happened. Who killed your husband?"

Blood drips steadily onto the soft white padding at Mrs. Johnson's feet. She lifts the torn fingers to her mouth and drinks from the wounds, letting little rivulets of crimson draw lines down her chin. "I ran to the porch when I heard them shouting…."

"Who was shouting?" Doctor Kendrick asks softly.

"There was so much blood. I ran into the porch and that demon was screaming and kicking. My husband, Jerry. . ." Her voice trails off into a tear-filled sob. "Jerry was trying to hold the boy down but he was too strong."

"What happened next, Mrs. Johnson? I need to know about the boy."

"He pushed us away and then dove through the table," she says with finality.

Doctor Kendrick looks to the orderly and then back to the deranged woman. "What do you mean? How did he dive through the table?"

"He yelled 'de profundis' and then his body jerked through the glass table and he disappeared. Fletcher just vanished." Mrs. Johnson turns her head up and stares directly into Lissa's eyes. "The demons inside his body took him. That boy is possessed."

"De profundis," she mouths the Latin phrase to herself. Doctor Kendrick shakes her head and stands, ready to leave the room. "You said that there was a lot of blood. Did someone get cut by the broken glass?"

"No," she sighs and looks at the cushioned ceiling. "Jerry didn't get cut on the glass. I was holding him and we both cried. . ." Her eyes are vacant, consumed by the horror of the memory. "He just fell apart in my arms. His body disintegrated and crumbled in my arms."

The orderly lets out a heavy sigh and opens the door for Doctor Kendrick to leave. The frazzled Mrs. Johnson curls up in the corner of the padded cell and begins sobbing.

Gehenna: a place without time.

I claw my way through the dusty ground, inch after painful inch. The whip strikes my back with every pathetic step that I manage to take. I keep my head down and my eyes shut tightly, trying not to flinch from the ear shattering cracks or the searing pain. I can hear laughter and get the distinct feeling that I am being herded. With a quick jerk of my head, I manage to glance ahead of me, but all I can see is an endless world of dirt and sand. I continue forward and despite my deepest desires, my consciousness refuses to slip away.

After hours of the grueling torture, the dusty grime beneath my fingers gives way to shattered concrete. A church bell tolls one solemn note and I lift my head from the ground.

My world changes in an instant. Pain spreads like fire from my lower back and cascades throughout my entire body in dreadful pulses. I am lying face down on a large slab of broken pavement that smells like hot lead and sulfur.

The ground vibrates and broken bits of concrete jump like breadcrumbs all around me. I pull myself to my knees and survey the area, looking for any signs of safety. Plaster and debris shower down from the ruins of an old building and clouds my vision. The street is long, lined with urban buildings on both sides that are barely standing. Gaping holes pockmark the storefronts and every window I can see holds no glass. The vibration in the ground grows, shaking loose big chunks of the nearest buildings. I scramble backward, hitting my torn back against a brick wall before turning and darting through a ruined doorway.

A boy, younger than me by a few years, cowers under a broken table. He holds a finger to his lips and motions for me to join him. My eyes dart around the room, a kitchen of sorts, and I notice black streaks and evidence of fire everywhere. The boy reaches out and touches my hand, pulling me close. The skin of his palm is rough and cut in many places with burns that ooze puss.

I crouch beneath the table and wait. The vibration is strong enough to make my teeth chatter and my vision blur. The boy covers his ears just as a string of deafening gunshots skip along the pavement where I previously crawled.

"Who is shooting?" I whisper, but the boy doesn't respond. I can't hear my own voice above the noise of the automatic gunfire. Bullets chew through the brick of the house and turn everything into a cloud of black debris. The boy closes his eyes and puts his head between his legs as the gunfire creeps closer. Small, jagged, pieces of the kitchen floor splatter our hiding spot and give me hundreds of microscopic cuts on my naked body.

The intensity of the vibration plateaus and a dark green cylinder destroys what remained of the kitchen wall just a couple of feet in front of me. The metal cylinder is immediately followed by a matching green tank that rolls through the rubble with ease. It stops, half on the broken pavement and half in the kitchen, and for a brief instant, the world is quiet.

Fire blasts from the turret and I can feel the heat singeing the hairs on my body. A hurricane of lead rains down upon the tank, sending bullets ricocheting all around the kitchen. The tank begins moving forward, absorbing the gunfire without pause, and the turret adjusts slightly to the right. It stops again and fires. The ensuing explosion brings an end to the hail of gunfire and the tank rolls away, continuing down the street. I can hear one of the buildings crumbling to ruins in the distance.

"What's going on?" I ask the boy who saved my life. He looks at me and his eyes become wide with terror.

"What's happening? Where am I?" I ask him, desperate for answers. He kicks me harshly in the side and bolts from under the table.

"Amerikaner! Amerikaner!" he shouts with an outstretched finger pointing at me. The boy is wearing a khaki colored shirt tucked into dark green shorts that remind me of a military uniform.

"Yes, I am American," I tell him, crawling out from under the table. I extend a hand and try to introduce myself. "My name is Fletcher Lee," I say. "I'm from Ohio. What's your name?"

The boy screams "Amerikaner!" again, practically shrieking the word, and draws a grey knife from his belt.

I put my hands in the air and take a defensive step backward. Broken tiles and shattered bits of brick crunch beneath my bare feet and dig into my skin. "Who are you?" I yell at him through gritted teeth. I'm defenseless and don't understand the situation.

"Für unser Führer!" The boy screams again. He flips the knife around in his hand, raises it high above his head, and charges.

"No!" I yell back at him. I turn and stumble over broken chair legs and shattered bricks. A jagged edge of cement cuts painfully into my knee but I have to keep going. The boy's heavy boots crunch into the broken glass right behind me. I scramble over a destroyed window frame and fall to the other side on my feet. The black pavement is hot on my bare skin and stings. The boy is chasing me, climbing through the window at my back and nearly upon me. I run down the war-torn street as fast as I can, but I can see other children, young kids like me, standing in the ruins. Most of them are dressed like the boy I met in the kitchen.

"Why are you chasing me?" I scream out of frustration. Some of the other children lining the street push through the rubble and start walking toward me. One of them is holding a gun but she doesn't raise it.

I can hear gunshots in the distance, somewhere far behind me, accented by the periodic retort of thunderous tank fire. Fire burns in the empty husk of a ruined vehicle that blocks my path. The only way out is through the charred remains of the homes and businesses that surround me, but they are filled with grimy children I cannot trust.

I turn in the street and feel the heat from the burning car warming my back. The boy that was chasing me stops at arm's length and points with his knife. "Amerikaner!" he yells in my face. "Ein Spion!" he shouts, and the other children come out of the rubble to encircle me. I look around at them, pleading with my eyes for understanding, but the horde is silent.

"What do you want from me?" I cry. All I can think about is covering my nakedness, but my eyes are fixed on the gleaming point of steel aimed at my chest. To raucous cheers from the crowd of children, the boy rushes me. His eyes burn red like fire and he growls, baring his teeth like a rabid dog.

I catch his wrist with my hand, turning the blade down before it skewers my gut. His body collides with mine and we both fall to the ground. He is smaller than me and probably younger by at least a few years but underneath him, I don't have enough room to gain any leverage.

Little teeth bite down into the meat of my shoulder and the kid flails wildly, dropping the knife and using his fists to pummel my ribcage. I clamp my arms down tightly over my chest, trying to protect myself, and jerk my chin into the boy's head. He yelps, but doesn't give up. I hit him again with my chin and he pulls his head back. I can see his eyes searching for the blade among the ruins.

My hand comes up around his neck and I squeeze, using my longer arms to keep his flailing body at bay. With a groan, I am able to put my feet beneath me and stand, easily overpowering the youngster. The boy smiles and I know that he has found the knife again. Without hesitation or the slightest thought of consequences, I tighten my grip on his throat and punch. His nose gives way in a torrent of blood beneath my knuckles.

The crowd of children screams for more and my rage boils, begging what remains of my conscience to hit him again. He clutches at his broken nose, holding the leather hilt over the wound. I let go of his neck and grab him firmly by his forearms, attempting to calm him down and hold him still. For all of my anger, I don't want to hurt him.

He looks at me with soft blue eyes devoid of the fiery rage I saw just moments before and I can tell that he is defeated.

An explosion rattles the building to my left, drawing everyone's attention. The strong vibration and deafening shockwave make me clutch to the kid for support. He pulls back and my hand slips, ripping a red and white armband off of the boy's khaki uniform. I stumble backward and my head hits part of the burning metal car, cutting a deep gash in the back of my skull that oozes blood. I scream out in pain and push away from the burning vehicle. I can smell the skin on my left palm melting from the heat.

A storm of uncontrollable fury rises in my chest and all I can see is a vision of my hands tearing the life from the boy in front of me. I leap onto him, feeling nothing but adrenaline and I relish wave after wave of violent ire. A chunk of black pavement is in my hands but I don't remember picking it up. I strike the boy in the head and the crowd of children around me grows silent. The distant ticking of bullets and the gentle crackle of fire are the only sounds that accompany my unhallowed slaughter.

The fearful rage I once saw in the young boy's eyes takes over my body. I roar into the face of the mangled corpse and let the body fall from my hands. Looking around the street, I am prepared to fight the other children as well, but I am alone.

I try to wipe the blood from my hands, but I am naked and surrounded only by the meager comforts of war. I steal the boy's leather boots and knife and start down the street, looking for refuge.

Laughter rings out in the darkest reaches of my mind, and though I feel sick to my stomach from what I have just done, a smile creeps onto my face.

Tuesday, November 9th, 1976

Doctor Kendrick comes to a stop on the curb outside of the Lee residence. The house looks empty in the waning evening light. Rich Lee's car isn't in the driveway but a nagging feeling that she is being watched makes the hairs on Lissa's neck stand on end. She inspects each of the windows from the safety of her vehicle before collecting her thoughts and opening the car door.

The concrete pathway leading up to Mrs. Johnson's house is neatly trimmed and everything about the house gives off an air of perfection. Not a branch is out of place on the row of tall green hedges that garnish the house's finely painted exterior.

Her expensive high-heeled shoes dig into the soft, neatly cut grass of the Johnson's side yard. Yellow police tape covers the windows and doors, reminding Lissa of a haunted house that kids need to pay to walk through. She shudders, thinking about what happened inside the porch. The air behind the house is cool and she pulls the white lab coat tight around her shoulders. A stiff breeze raises goose bumps on her skin.

Doctor Kendrick pushes her face against the wire screen and sees the empty metal table frame. A dark spot remains on the wooden floor where someone tried to clean up a large amount of blood. There is a wooden door leading into the screened-in porch and Lissa tries the handle, only to find it locked.

Using a pen from her lab coat pocket, she pries an edge of the screen paneling open just enough to slide her hand through and unlock the door from the inside. The hinges squeak as the door opens, making Doctor Kendrick take a frightened step back. She grabs the doorframe and tries to steady her breathing, but the growing shadows fill her with dread. The sun is at her back and falling quickly, she reminds herself.

Summoning her courage, she steps onto the creaking wood floor and quickly hurries around the broken table. Bits of glass still litter the floor and one of the wicker chairs is on its side. She bends down to inspect the dark stain on the deck when a sharp scraping noise catches her attention so forcefully that she nearly tumbles over.

"Chairs cannot move on their own," she says loudly to herself. "That chair was propped against the screen when I got here." Her voice shakes and her statements do little to comfort her mind. She turns her attention back to the dark stain, eager to be finished.

The substance is still a little sticky to the touch and comes off almost black on her fingertips. She smells it and immediately reacts to the acrid stench. "Dark chocolate…" she whispers, bringing her nose as close to the spot as possible. The chair propped against the screen slams back into the wooden floor.

Lissa screams with terror, falling back against the wall of the house and frantically trying to put as much room between her and the chair. "It is the wind," she repeats a dozen times to herself. "Just the wind." In the back of her mind, she knows she is lying.

With her eyes closed tightly to the shadows, Doctor Kendrick bends over the dark substance one more time and wafts the scent to her nostrils. "Dark chocolate and… Cedar?" she asks with a quizzical look. She looks around the room for any more of the sticky substance but the rest of the room is immaculately clean.

The chair moves again, turning as if someone is sliding it against the wooden floor to watch Doctor Kendrick. The tall woman stands and runs from the porch, falling through the door and yelling with fright.

"Hey, are you alright?" a male voice calls to her. She hears footsteps rapidly approaching and tries to compose herself.

"Doctor Kendrick?" The voice belongs to Rich Lee. Lissa stand, her legs visibly trembling with fear, and attempts to brush the hair from her face and look dignified.

Fletcher's dad jogs up to her and places a hand on her shoulder, leaning too close for Doctor Kendrick to feel comfortable. "I'm quite fine, thank you," she tells him curtly and takes a step away. "I was just. . ." she tries to find the right words. "Looking for clues as to where your son might have gone."

Rich hangs his head with sorrow but Doctor Kendrick can

easily tell that the gesture is half-hearted at best. "The police said that he just disappeared, like he ran away or something. I feel like I never even knew my own kid."

A chill runs the length of Lissa's spine and makes her shiver but the wind is calm. "Why don't we go next door to your house and talk about it?"

Rich smiles and attempts to place his arm around her as they walk, but Doctor Kendrick speeds past him as hastily as she can with her impractical footwear.

Lissa Kendrick sits down on a light green sofa as Rich stands awkwardly in front of the kitchen refrigerator and offers her a drink. She politely turns it down with a wave of her hand. "You seem to be awfully at ease with the disappearance of your son, Mr. Lee," she says curtly.

Rich sits down on one of the room's wooden chairs and crosses his feet on the short coffee table. He folds his hands on his chest over his dark leisure suit and lets out a prolonged sigh. "It pains me that you would say that, Doctor Kendrick, it truly pains me."

"Why is that? If I had a son that went missing at a crime scene, I would be tearing the city apart looking for him." Doctor Kendrick sits on the edge of the couch with her back straight, nervously smoothing the wrinkles of her outfit under her lab coat. The house makes her feel uneasy, like she is being watched by something she cannot see.

"But you have no son, Doctor Kendrick, and you will certainly never have a son like Fletcher, so you don't know what it is like, do you?" The calm tone of Rich's voice reveals nothing. He stares at Lissa with half of a smile embedded into a blank expression.

"What do you mean?" she asks, letting her shoulders relax slightly.

"Fletcher. . ." Rich sighs, shaking his head. "Where do I begin? Fletcher is a strange child. Incredibly introverted. All he ever wanted to do was play with the dog or read. I tried to get him into sports and other normal activities for kids his age but he didn't take to them."

"Lots of boys are introverted and prefer solitude to the company of their peers." Doctor Kendrick manages a smile and brushes her fingers through her blonde hair. "I was just like that growing up. My parents would lock me out of the house in order to force me to play with the other children."

"Yes," Rich continues, "Fletcher is like that. He doesn't speak much and according to his first doctor, he might have some sort of social anxiety disorder or emotional disability." He waves his hand at the idea as though the entire science of psychology is nonsense. "We never wanted to put him on any medicine, you know, we didn't want to screw with his brain."

"I have certainly met many parents who feel the same way, Mr. Lee. And though it may not always be my professional judgment to withhold medication, I am always in favor of counseling and therapy in place of drugs."

Rich nods, thankful for the support. "My wife, Melinda, she always said that if God made Fletcher the way he is, then that is how he is going to be. I can't rightly say that I disagree with that philosophy myself. God doesn't create problems, she would tell me, He only makes opportunities." Solemn tears well up in the corners of Rich's eyes, the first real sign of emotion he has shown to Doctor Kendrick.

"I'm sorry for your loss, Mr. Lee, but please, I am here about Fletcher and his safety. If you could tell me what you know about his possible whereabouts—"

Rich cuts her off in a sudden outburst of anger. "You think I know where my son is? You think I know that and I just sit here and talk to you like nothing is wrong?" he shouts, forcing Doctor Kendrick back onto the couch with his posturing.

"I didn't mean—" she stammers, cut off again.

"I know exactly what you meant by it!" Rich settles back down into his seat and hangs his head in embarrassment. "I'm sorry," he tells her weakly, fighting past the lump in his throat. "I shouldn't yell."

"I understand, Mr. Lee. These are trying times for you and your family. I just want to do anything I can to get Fletcher back safely." Doctor Kendrick looks at Rich with a warm smile, trying to comfort him, but he doesn't meet her gaze.

"If I knew where Fletcher ran off to, I would go there myself to get him," Rich says through a suppressed sob.

"Mr. Lee. . ." Doctor Kendrick clears her throat, unsure how to proceed. "Do you know much about the occult?" He looks up at her with a confused expression. "Demons, devils, angels, Heaven and Hell;

do you believe in those sorts of things?"

"No," he says quickly, but then hesitates. "Well, I believe what little I've read in the Bible, like an angel visiting Mary and telling her the news, but demons and devils? Melinda was the religious one, not me. I don't know much about that sort of thing."

"Fletcher certainly believed in demons, Mr. Lee," she states with a heavy air of seriousness.

"What do you mean?"

"Your son told me things, disturbing things, about a demon that he witnessed on a regular basis." Doctor Kendrick scoots forward and her eyes scan the shadows of the room, looking for glimpses of anything surreal.

After a long silence, Rich shakes his head and whispers. "The man from the shadows?" he asks quietly, grasping his hands together as if in prayer.

"Yes," Lissa replies, matching his quiet tone. "Fletcher described him to me as a man without features, without a face. What did he tell you?"

"The boy would tell me horrible things, disturbing things, things no child should ever have to hear, much less say. That's the reason the school kicked him out. He told the other students about the man from the shadows watching them and sitting next to them, it was too much for a lot of them to handle." Rich wipes his cheek with the sleeve of his suit and takes a deep breath.

"You never believed him, did you?" Doctor Kendrick asks, fearing the answer.

"Would you?"

Wednesday, November 10th, 1976

Lissa Kendrick sits in the back pew of Saint Timothy's Episcopal Church and watches the late night vesper service with silent respect. Candles adorn the wooden altar and a pungent smell wafting from a censer fills the air. Only a handful of parishioners sit in the uncomfortable pews late on a Wednesday night and it makes the church feel hollow and unwelcoming.

After an hour long sermon and few stanzas of unfamiliar chanting, Doctor Kendrick is finally able to make her way to the office at the front of the sanctuary.

"I was glad to see you in church tonight, Doctor," Pastor Santiago says as he ushers her into the cramped office.

"It has been a long time since I have attended services anywhere," she tells him. The office is just as she remembers, poorly lit and covered with stacks of books.

"Please, have a seat and tell me: what brings you to Saint Timothy's tonight? I heard the news about Fletcher's disappearance. . ." he says sadly. "He will be dearly missed."

"Pastor Santiago," she clears her throat and collects her thoughts. "Something that Mrs. Johnson, Fletcher's neighbor, told me in the hospital bothers me. She described Fletcher's vanishing as though he was pulled by something invisible in the room and dragged through the top of a glass patio table."

The old man takes a moment to think before responding. "You want to know if some sort of astral body might have captured the boy?"

"You took the question right out of my mind, Pastor," Lissa says. "Is that possible? You'll have to forgive me, Pastor; I hardly know anything about this sort of occurrence."

"I do not believe that any sort of demon would be capable of coming to our plane of existence and stealing a human." He shakes his head and rubs tiredness from his eyes. "The Bible talks about possession and demonic influences here on earth, and even mentions visitation by angels, but nowhere in that book does a demon go to earth and simply steal a child."

"The woman and her husband were trying to restrain Fletcher. The boy was in some kind of rage or mania, kicking and yelling. He said the phrase 'de profundis' right before he broke the table and vanished. I think it was Latin, do you have any idea what it means?" Pastor Santiago's expression is grave, giving Lissa all the answer she needs.

"You're correct. That phrase means 'from the depths.' It usually refers to Psalm 130 which says 'From the depths, I have cried out to you, O Lord.' In this case, I fear that it might refer to something else altogether."

"What do you mean?" Doctor Kendrick asks, fighting a fresh wave of fear that assaults her from every hidden shadow in the room.

"That inscription was often used in medieval times by Satanists and other crazed demon worshipers. Historical scholars on the subject have agreed that the words 'de profundis' would appear at the end of a ritual in which a demonic presence was successfully summoned to this world. Of course, none of it can be proven." Pastor Santiago digs through a deep pocket of his robe and takes out a small metal crucifix and lays it on the table. "If what you say is true, and the stories from the old days about demonic summoning have any hint of accuracy, it would be best that you take no risks."

Doctor Kendrick picks the crucifix up from the table and inspects it, marveling at the detail in the pain on Christ's face. "You said it isn't possible for demons to come to our plane. How will this help?"

"Unfortunately for both of us, I do not hold all of the answers. Just because the Bible doesn't say that something is possible, that does not force us to assume that it is impossible. As Martin Luther often said, God purposely withholds information from humanity and the Bible is not the complete story of theology, but it is rather all that God is willing to tell us." The old man stands to usher her from the office, but Lissa doesn't move.

"Pastor, there is one more thing I would like to ask you," she says, placing the crucifix in her pocket. "The censer that holds the burning incense, what is it for?"

The robed man stares at her for a long moment before answering. "It is tradition to spread clouds of incense throughout the church during our vesper services. Why do you ask? Does the smoke bother you?"

"It is just that. . ." Doctor Kendrick searches her mind for the right words. "The last time I was here, I smelled something else. It was a sweet cedar smell, not incense. I smelled the same thing on the porch where Fletcher vanished." Pastor Santiago places his hands forcefully on the table and leans over the doctor in a menacing manner. She pushes her chair back and nervously looks around the room, visibly frightened.

"Describe to me exactly what you smelled, Doctor Kendrick," he growls more than asks.

"It was like strong cedar mixed with the aroma of dark chocolate…" she whispers. "I remember it because it was so pleasant."

Pastor Santiago turns on his heel, sending his black robe flying out in a wide arc behind him. "Follow me," he commands. The man bends at the waist and pulls one of the musty stacks of books out from the corner of the office. A small wooden panel is set into the brick which he quickly removes. Santiago reaches a hand deep into the opening and a strange series of clicks and scrapes sound somewhere overhead.

The wall behind the pastor's desk rises up on heavy chains that remind Doctor Kendrick of a rollercoaster ascending the first hill. A wrought iron, tightly spiraled staircase leading down into utter darkness awaits them. Pastor Santiago only glances over his shoulder once to make sure that Doctor Kendrick is following him.

As soon as the two are fully on the staircase, Santiago releases a hook in the stone passageway that lowers the false wall back into place. The air is cool and Doctor Kendrick knows that they are descending underground. She tries to count the steps to determine the depth, but loses track after five stories in pitch darkness.

Finally, Pastor Santiago stops at the bottom of the staircase and fumbles in his robe for a large iron key. The door swings silently open on heavy, well-oiled hinges and reveals a long hallway lit by low burning coals in metal braziers. The holy man takes a few small sticks from a bundle next to the doorway and tosses them on the nearest brazier, making the embers spark to life and illuminate the passage.

"I feel like I am in a secret passage under a medieval castle," Doctor Kendrick remarks, admiring the beauty of the precise masonry. She reaches out and brushes her fingertips against the dark stone. Tiny dew droplets coat the hewn walls and shimmer in the light of the fires.

"This church was built long before any of the European settlers that most people are familiar with ever landed on the east coast." Doctor Kendrick stands a full head taller than the pastor but still finds no reason to duck in the underground corridor. She gazes up at the ceiling and can make out intricately carved wooden beams intersecting the rocks and forming delicate patterns.

"The ceiling," she points to the nearest wooden beam. "I feel like I remember these symbols. . ." Doctor Kendrick stops and tilts her head back to better inspect the carvings. "Yes, I remember them from something in my childhood; something that I learned in school perhaps." She hurries her gait to catch up with the pastor who shakes his head.

"I doubt it," the old man says, reaching deeper into his robe and producing another heavy, iron key. "Only a few scholars have been permitted to study this entryway and by their conclusion, the symbols you see inscribed in the wooden beams are ancient Swedish runes." He turns the key in the door and two large, metal bars clang to the ground on the other side. "The language of the Vikings," he tells her with a smile as the door swings open.

Doctor Kendrick takes a step back to allow the pastor to enter the next room first. "I may have lived my adult life here in the Midwest," she grins with mild arrogance, "but I was born in northern Sweden to a father who worked as a historian for the state."

Pastor Santiago nods his head and chuckles to himself. "Something has to explain your pale skin and blonde hair."

"Don't forget, Viking women have to be tall in order to give birth to strong Viking warlords," she jests.

"This room wasn't even discovered until just a few hundred years ago," the pastor says, returning the serious timbre to his voice. "No one was sure what it was used for until the last couple of decades." The room beyond the Viking entrance hall is circular, lit by smoldering coals, and contains only one low, cylindrical pillar of stone.

"Do I even want to know what the purpose of this table is?" Doctor Kendrick wonders aloud. Images of brutal human sacrifice flash through her mind. A thick layer of black ooze coats the low stone table and the smell is overwhelmingly strong.

"Cedar and dark chocolate?" Pastor Santiago laughs. "I have never heard it described like that, though I suppose you are right." He walks around the circular table and lifts a monstrously large tome from the floor, letting it slam onto the black ooze with a loud clap.

"Most of these pages are written in the same runic language as the beams outside," he explains, casually flipping through the dusty sheets, "but some of them are in other, more easily translated languages. Some forms of Hebrew and Aramaic are present, along with something that could easily by Egyptian from the time of the Exodus, and the last few pages are all written in neatly penned Latin." With a great sigh born from years of frustration, Pastor Santiago closes the book.

"What is it?" Doctor Kendrick asks, astounded. "What does the book say?"

"Most of what has been translated doesn't make any sense," he says with defeat. "The Latin phrases are all just two or three word maxims, many of which the average American would recognize without hesitation. Long lists of symbols accompany each phrase but to my knowledge, the order of the lists isn't always right."

"What do you mean? Is it some sort of code?" Lissa moves around the table to inspect the book, turning the stiff pages with reverence.

"You can think of it like that, I guess," Santiago responds. "Consider this book to be a journal." He points out the different types of paper used in the construction of the tome as he speaks. "Look, it can be assumed that your Swedish ancestors compiled the thing, but from a plethora of sources that span millennia. Have you ever heard of alchemy?"

Doctor Kendrick looks at him with confusion. "Like, medieval wizards turning people into frogs and lead into gold?"

The robed man laughs heartily and puts a hand on Lissa's shoulder. "Lead into gold, certainly, but people into frogs? That kind of alchemy is only in the movies. Only a handful of people living today even know that this book exists and still fewer have laid eyes on it. What we have come to believe, is that this tome is the collected journals of several of history's greatest alchemists. The traditional goal of alchemy, as portrayed especially by film and literature, is the conquest of the elements and the attainment of wealth," he explains.

"That sounds like most of the people I have ever met, Pastor. What makes an alchemist so special?"

Pastor Santiago nods vigorously, enjoying his role as teacher. "Alchemists sought not only to master the scholastic disciplines of chemistry and physics; they also strove to understand the divine realms of existence." He flips to a section near the back of the book and points to several Latin inscriptions. "The further into the book you go, the closer to modern times the scripts become. What is frightening is that the last several authors only chose to concern themselves with the alchemical art of summoning." His finger traces a line through the text and taps on the phrase 'de profundis' etched in neat black ink.

"From the depths," Doctor Kendrick whispers, suddenly aware of every shadow in the small, dark room.

"About fourteen years ago, there was a break-in at the church," Pastor Santiago explains grimly. Lissa's mind races, thinking back to the story of Fletcher's birth.

"When I got down here to make sure that everything was in order," he continues gravely, "I found the book open to this page and all of the symbols listed next to the phrase had been drawn in the black ooze on the table."

A long silence passes between the two and shadows of fear come alive in Doctor Kendrick's mind. "Did they ever find the people who broke in?" she finally manages to ask.

"Not to this day," the pastor utters with a cold shiver. "There are other passages in the book that refer directly to Hell, and the word 'profundis' is never specifically translated from Biblical texts to mean anything other than suffering or torment, so I can't be sure what kind of ritual was performed here on that night. What I can assure you is that whatever took place, the people who broke into the church were not trying to bring angels into the world."

"Pastor. . ." Doctor Kendrick hesitates, hardly believing the conclusions that her mind is drawing. "I don't think this particular phrase is about summoning." She runs her fingers along the page, feeling the lines of ink beneath her skin. "Would it be possible for this ritual to open a gateway of some sort between planes of existence?"

Santiago ponders the question and shrugs. "I suppose that it can, although without any records, it cannot be proven one way or the other."

"Mrs. Johnson told me that Fletcher dove through the glass table, but the fact remains that she and her husband were trying to restrain him. Two grown adults, even their age, should be able to pin down one 13-year-old boy with ease." Her mind conjures up frightful images of the featureless man that Fletcher described to her and she shudders, closing her eyes to the shadows. "What if the . . . demon . . . that Fletcher sees grabbed hold of him and used the glass tabletop as a portal?"

"Do you think that Fletcher is, right now, in some otherworldly depth of sorrow?" The low flames in the nearest brazier waver and threaten to go out.

"I don't know, but if he is," Doctor Kendrick declares with confident resolve, "I intend to get him out."

Gehenna: a place without time.

I awaken in my own bed, safe under the warm covers. I can hear my dad getting dressed in his room and quietly talking to himself as though nothing is wrong. He must not know what has happened. I slip out of the sheets and pad down the hallway, checking every shadow that I pass for signs of evil.

The kitchen is brightly lit, much brighter than I have ever seen it. Buzzing fluorescent lights cover the ceiling and large, round surgical lamps point at me from every angle. I know that I am still lost and my world is controlled by the featureless man.

I sit down at the kitchen table and wait for whatever may come, closing my eyes to the piercing light. The chair across from me scrapes against the shiny linoleum floor and someone, presumably my dad, sits down.

"Fletcher," I hear her voice like sunshine breaking through an azure sky choked by stormy clouds.

"Mom?" I jerk my head up from the table, wanting nothing more than to see her alive and well. My gut churns and bile rises in my throat. It is her, of that I am sure. She is wearing the exact same outfit that I found her hanging in, even the blood-splattered burlap sack over her face.

"Mom . . ." I whisper, turning my head away. "Why?"

She stands from the table, reaching a hand to my shoulder and beckoning for me to follow her. I can hear the whip cracking in the back of my mind and I know that I have no choice. I am being herded again; the very thought of such control makes a fresh dose of rage form in the pit of my stomach.

Reluctantly, I stand to follow her. She reaches a hand behind her back, inviting me to take it, but I don't. She leads me out of the house at a fast pace, nearly jogging. I struggle to keep up and trip over the base of one of the lamps. My mom turns and catches me, spinning so quickly that she must have known I would trip before my foot struck the metal.

"Thanks," I mutter, but it feels awkward to speak to a corpse. Her head turns, pushing the corners of the burlap sack, and I can feel her gaze. For a moment I can forget the rope pulled tightly around her neck and the thick, red blood seeping from the woven burlap.

The serenity breaks and she bolts out of the front door with her arms flailing in the air. She stops in the middle of the front yard and falls to her knees slowly and dramatically. I watch her from the concrete walkway that leads to the front door and wonder what is happening. My back still aches from the whipping I endured and I can still feel the broken, war torn pavement under my feet.

She turns and raises a delicate hand, pointing at the large window set into the front of the house. Shadows swarm all around my feet like a million tiny scarabs smothering the ground. Frantically stomping my feet to keep the black incorporeal beetles at bay, I turn to follow my mom's pointing finger. The scarabs rush at the house and pour through the window as I watch in horror. The light I tripped over rocks back and forth precariously. All I can hear is laughter.

The light falls to the floor, shattering on impact, and spreading a line of fire onto the shag carpet. The fire is small at first, but spreads steadily to consume the entire kitchen. My dad walks into the room, groggily rubbing the sleep from his eyes. I run up to the window and slam my fists onto it, screaming. With his back turned to the flames, he tips the coffee pot down to the edge of his mug. I yell at him, striking the glass over and over, trying to get his attention, but he never sees me.

He turns around and drops the coffee cup out of fright, spilling the dark liquid all over his legs. Panic overwhelms him and smoke begins to fill the room. The fire climbs over the electrical cords attached to the circular lamps all over the room and spreads rapidly. Wallpaper curls and falls to the ground in clumps of blackened ash.

No matter how much he stomps on the flames, they only grow stronger. I watch as my dad fights the fires but I know that he is doomed. The window cracks and releases a burst of heat into my face that smells like death. I rip at the glass, throwing my fists into it with wild abandon, finally making a hole large enough to crawl through. The room is full of thick, black smoke that stings my eyes. I clench a hand over my mouth to help me breathe but it does little more than bring a meager, intangible comfort.

I try to pull the hem of my shirt up enough to cover my face but my hand touches only skin. I look down and my mother laughs from the yard; again, I find myself naked and am ashamed. The fire hasn't killed my dad yet and I know that I can get to him and save him.

Standing on the inside of the window, surrounded by licking flames and watching my dad's clothes and hair ignite, all I can think about is hiding my nakedness. I cower behind the burning couch, feeling the skin on my arms begin to boil. Large red spots develop all over my body. They bubble and grow, eventually cracking and releasing blood and puss. The fires continue to strengthen all around me and though my body burns, I do not lose consciousness like my dad. He falls to the ground and kicks for a few long seconds, but then becomes still. His chest continues to rise and fall with his breathing but his back spasms with every ragged gasp.

My mom looks at me through the bloody burlap, standing on the recently mowed lawn, and laughs. "Fletcher," she says, and the voice comes from all around, as though the fire itself is speaking. "You tripped. This fire is yours. There is blood on your hands, Fletcher, and not just daddy's."

I want to scream and run to her and hit her for what she says but the fires block my path. I can't breathe and when I close my lungs to the world, they burn but do not fail. Pain becomes my very existence, filling my thoughts and devouring my mind. I watch in horror as the skin from my forearm sloughs onto the burning carpet and smolders. Bands of red muscle pop and sizzle in the fire, exploding in pain with every movement I make.

"Save me!" I finally manage to yell although my jaw falls to the floor in the process. I can taste my own ashes in my mouth. The house is blazing so furiously that all I can see of my mom is her dark, laughing silhouette.

I try to grab the back of the couch and pull myself toward the window but my arms rip free of their sockets and the cloth couch crumbles into a heap of burning embers. "Save me!" I try to scream again. Nothing more than the hissing sounds of evaporating water escape my ruined mouth.

One feeble attempt at a step and my knees buckle, submitting to the heat, and I fall to the ground. My face is buried in the burning floor. From the corner of my eye, I can see my dad's remnants scuttling away like tumbleweeds in the desert wind.

"If you weren't so concerned with yourself, you could have saved him, Fletcher." My mom's voice drips with mockery. Guilt overwhelms me and I know that she is right.

Friday, November 12th, 1976

"How do we find out if Fletcher Lee has been captured by some otherworldly entity?" Doctor Kendrick asks the room full of experts. Pastor Santiago stands next to her wearing his customary black robe tied about his waist with a simple length of braided rope.

"I say it is impossible!" A man wearing a nice suit and a bronze monocle exclaims. Pastor Santiago introduced him as a professor and expert of ancient and medieval theology. "Everything that we know from the old demonology texts is nothing more than untested hypothesis!"

"Then perhaps it is time that we test some of these ideas. Wouldn't you agree, professor?" A man standing in the back of the room chimes in. He is tall, with greasy black hair sticking out from underneath a sheepskin hat that reminds Lissa of raven's wings. His name is Wilfred Montesquieu, but everyone refers to him as 'The Money.' The Montesquieu family estate owns the rights to a dozen or more bed and breakfast hotels as well as various high class restaurants all over the world. Wilfred single-handedly funds the entire Society for the Theological Exploration of the Unknown.

"Need I remind you, gentlemen, that this organization is strictly *against* dabbling with these sorts of rituals?" Pastor Santiago, as the host and one of the founding members of the society, held a highly valued opinion that was obviously respected.

"There are other means," The Money responds. "I am not suggesting that we try to perform one of these arcane rituals ourselves, I am merely entertaining the idea of either finding someone who has, or paying someone to do it for us." The gathering of men erupts into excited chatter. Everyone, it seems, has a very strong opinion.

Doctor Kendrick holds up a hand to quiet the room. "Gentlemen, please!" she shouts over them, gathering everyone's attention.

"Remember, there is a human life, a child's life, at stake here. We need to at least be open-minded enough to *consider* every possibility." She turns to Wilfred and gestures for him to come forward. "Now, if you would be so kind . . ."

The Money tips the gray fabric of his hat in appreciation and spreads his arms wide to address the small gathering. "We need to look at every piece of information available to us," he begins with a charismatic smile. "The strange and unfortunate events surrounding Fletcher's birth, coinciding perfectly with the break in that occurred at this very church, cannot be ignored. We have the *Keys of Solomon*," he states, pointing a finger in the direction of the professor.

"It seems that one of our guests brought a little more than just his own skin with him," Pastor Santiago jests under his breath. Doctor Kendrick's stomach churns with nausea.

"We know the names of these supposed demons and, according to the alchemists of old, we can use that to control them, should the need arise." Another burst of energy from the society greets his idea and takes a long moment to calm down.

Doctor Kendrick's right hand is firmly grasped around the small metal crucifix in her pocket. Her eyes dart from shadow to shadow, nervously patrolling the undercroft of Saint Timothy's.

"That's just a myth . . ." she can hear Pastor Santiago utter from the corner of his mouth.

The Money raises his voice, commanding the attention of every ear in the room. "It is my suggestion that we decide on one of these rituals, go downstairs to the altar, and see what happens. If we succeed in opening a portal, we can decide what to do then. If we succeed in summoning a demon to our world, we can use the *Keys of Solomon* to control it and get the answers we seek. And if nothing at all happens," he turns and looks at Doctor Kendrick with a sly grin, "we will know that our missing boy has run off, and that his mental ailments have finally gotten the better of him."

Many of the gathered members of the society nod their heads in agreement, but the professor makes his way to the front of the room with a grim expression.

"Esteemed colleagues!" the old teacher addresses the group. "What is the primary reason for our society's existence? To *study* these supernatural and spiritual phenomena in the light of history and rigorous theological discourse! We have remained hidden from the world for so long because we do not dabble in magic and rituals. We leave that nonsense to the pagans with their book of spells."

"What does the 'de profundis' ritual require?" The Money asks, directing his question to Pastor Santiago. The robed man opens the heavy book to the last section and scans the pages for the appropriate phrase.

"If my Latin hasn't gotten too rusty over the long years spent since the seminary, I would say that not much is required." He glances at the doctor with a grim nod. "The list corresponding to the phrase 'de profundis' is as follows: darkness, an innocent person of strong Christian faith, and a demon . . . already present . . ."

The professor shakes his head and remains silent as all around him, the group excitedly jumps to conclusions and resumes their shouting. Pastor Santiago pounds his fist into the wooden podium that separates him from the rest of the society and gets them to quiet once more.

"This list is a far cry from the usual 'candles and blood' that appear next to most of the other phrases, but there is something more." Doctor Kendrick steps up beside the pastor and gazes down at the page. She can't read the Latin, but something in the Pastor's voice sets all of her nerves on edge. "Written to the side of the list in black ink, there seems to be a note, or some sort of addition." Pastor Santiago moves his finger under the words, translating them in his head with painstaking effort. "It says here that . . . the ritual requires certain . . . approval?"

With a few quick strides, Pastor Santiago takes the massive book to the professor and asks him for help. The two men confer on the meaning of the passage for a few minutes before Pastor Santiago returns to his position in front of the gathered men.

"This ritual requires the permission of the King of the West."

Much to Doctor Kendrick's surprise, and pleasure, the room is quiet. The various scholars whisper quietly among themselves before one of them, an old and wrinkled man wearing the robes of a pastor finally speaks out. "Asmodai?" he asks aloud, but the others shake their heads.

"Professor," The Money asks, "who is the King of the West, according to *The Keys of Solomon*?"

The wizened gentleman reaches into his leather briefcase and withdraws a package wrapped in thin, red silk. The book, reportedly bound in human flesh, is not nearly as large as the tome from the underground altar but appears to be thousands of years older. "If memory serves me right," he says while turning the yellowed pages, "the King of the West goes by the name Beliel, although some sources say that his real name is 'Gapp,' or 'Gorson,' or something like that."

Doctor Kendrick's breath catches in her throat and she nearly stumbles from shock. "Corson!" she yells out, stealing the focus of the room. "The King of the West is named Corson, with a 'C', not Gorson."

"And how, exactly, do you know this?" the professor asks with terse incredulity.

"How are you so positive?" The Money inquires.

Pastor Santiago places a hand on the tall woman's back to calm her down. "Fletcher said that his dog's name was Corson. He told me in one of our sessions and was very adamant about the spelling and pronunciation of the name."

"What does the kid's dog have to do with any of it?" The Money asks forcefully. All of the eyes in the room bore down on Doctor Kendrick, scrutinizing her intensely. "According to the story that Fletcher told me, the dog was the one who actually found his mother hanging from the rafters in the shed. The dog led him to her body."

"Well," The Money says with a new tone of seriousness in his voice. "That certainly changes things. I don't suppose that you asked the boy who named the dog, did you?"

"It never occurred to me at the time," Doctor Kendrick replies. "So, do we have a plan?"

The professor stands and turns to address the handful of other men in the room. "Although it pains me to say so, I believe that we have no choice. If the boy really did get involved in a demonic plot involving the King of the West, it is our duty as the only people properly educated in such matters to help the poor child." A low murmur of consent circulates through the members of the society.

"Do you think the dog was possessed?" Doctor Kendrick asks.

"The Bible tells us that animals are fully capable of being overcome by the spirits of the damned," Pastor Santiago explains. "I wouldn't be surprised if the boy's dog had been taken over by the presence of a malevolent spirit."

"Could it have been this King of the West, the demon named Corson from the *Keys of Solomon*?" Doctor Kendrick feels lost among the room full of well-educated theologians and historians. "I feel like I have to apologize, gentlemen, I am new to this entire . . ." she struggles to find the word, "field."

"I think that in this case, Doctor Kendrick," The Money responds, "you have it exactly right.  If the King of the West came up from hell in the body of a dog to plague the boy, I do not doubt that the ritual could have been completed by a lesser demon."

"So," Lissa asks quietly, "how do we go and get him out?"

Gehenna: a place without time.

The house lies in crumbled ruins all around me. I'm on my back, gazing into the bright blue sky, with the acrid smell of smoldering embers filling my nostrils. I curl my fingers into my palms and feel the muscles of my arms and back reacting. My body is whole and feels strong, without a single twang of pain despite the raging fire I had endured.

A hand reaches down from the corner of my vision and offers to lift me from the charred rubble. It is my mother's hand, extending from her lifeless, bloody corpse. I can't see her face through the burlap, but I can tell by her body language that she is smiling.

"Where am I?" I ask her once I am standing firmly on my feet. She holds onto my hand and turns, leading me out of the ruined house. We walk together over the debris and onto the street. My mom spreads her hands out wide, showing me the entire neighborhood. All of the houses that I remember are there, unaffected by my personal torments. She walks me down the street and points to a house I have never seen before.

The building, situated at the end of a picturesque cul-de-sac, is a massive structure of stone shaped like a castle. Large turrets flank either side of a big, modern looking garage door. I can see lights on in most of the rooms and the silhouette of a man talking on the phone and moving from room to room.

I make it to the front of the house and find the door unlocked. My mom stands behind me and ushers me into the castle. The foyer is immaculately gilded with two elegant marble staircases that wrap around the edges of the room. A golden fountain anchors the center of the room and tosses sweet smelling water into the air. Everything about the house drips with lavish opulence.

"What is this place?" I ask no one in particular, mindlessly running my fingers along the edge of the golden fountain.

"This is your home, my son." My mom says at my back. "Everything you see here is yours."

I continue to walk around the fountain and begin to ascend the marble staircase. The banister is made from dark mahogany accented by a solid gold gargoyle perched on the tightly spiraled terminus.

Elaborate oil paintings adorn the marble walls like plaques in a hall of fame. The first painting in the line is of me, as an infant, a picture I remember well from my house. The picture used to be in a cheap silver frame on our kitchen counter but here, it is a piece of art bordered by gold. More paintings of my childhood pictures line the walls all the way to the iron-banded double doors at the top of the curved staircase. All of the portraits are just of me; none of the other members of my family are present among the paintings.

I reach the top of the marble staircase and slowly open the heavy wooden door. The next room is a stark contrast to the opulent foyer that greeted my entry. The air is cold, frigid enough to see my breath. The heavy doors slam shut behind me and I have to swim through a field of hanging, plastic strips that hit against my shoulders.

The walls of the room are concrete, illuminated by caged fluorescent lights similar to the one I knocked over in my own house down the road. The crisp air is rapidly flowing, chopped by large overhead fans that add a disconcerting beat to the back of my mind. The chill wind is laced with hints of formaldehyde covering the unmistakable stench of death.

Thick steel chains dangle from the high ceiling and gently sway back and forth. Corpses writhe on the ends of the chains with brutal, rusty meat hooks protruding from patches of rotted flesh. All of the faces on the bodies are covered up by bloody burlap sacks. Strands of hemp rope tie the bags over their heads just like how I found my mom hanging in the shed. I turn back and look at her, and she leans over me like she always used to do. I imagine her smiling and telling me a story from her college sports days, but the animated corpse in front of me doesn't breathe.

"What is this place, mom?" I ask her. Her head turns upward and I can hear her face scrape against the bloody burlap.

"Don't be afraid, Fletcher Lee," is her only response. Why

would she use my last name? Why does she call me by my name at all and not a euphemism? Maybe it is the sickening stench meddling with my brain, but I can hardly think in the cold room. Nothing makes sense.

Her hand gently pushes into my back and I know that I am supposed to continue onward. I can see a white overhead door at the back of the room that I focus my gaze on, pushing past the dangling bodies. They bump into me and mindlessly scratch at my arms, not attacking, but curious as to what is walking among them. Hundreds of the bloody cadavers are hanging from the concrete ceiling in every direction.

I reach the center of the room and the corpses become more restless. Some of them nearest to me groan and lash out with their rotting hands. I break out into a run, knocking the corpses out of my path and slapping at their wrists to keep them at bay.

The corrugated overhead door is down, blocking my path. I turn, looking for my mom in the crowd of death, and I realize that every single body hanging from the rafters is a clone of her. All of the corpses, while dressed differently, are copies of my mom. Terror grips me and I am overcome by nauseated heaving. Whatever slimy substance was inside my stomach comes hurtling out, splattering across the cold grey floor.

I spot my mom walking through the sea of bodies. She is slowly making her way toward me, stopping at every corpse to gently caress it. Her head, covered in burlap, leans in close to one of the dangling bodies, and I can hear her quietly whispering. The speech is too soft to make out the words, but they sound comforting.

The flailing body immediately to my right grabs onto my arm, pulling at the skin and trying to rip the flesh from my bones. I slap at the hand but it grips tighter, relentlessly crushing my forearm. My mom is still a dozen rows of corpses away, taking her time to reach me. The dead fingers clutch like a vice. I thrash and pound the dangling corpse, trying to break free. When my mom finally reaches me, she whispers something to the violent body and it instantly calms, letting go of my arm and relaxing.

"Thank you," I tell my mom, wondering if she can understand me. Her soft hand reaches past my chest and touches the door which instantly responds. Belts crank above me and pull the overhead door up to the ceiling. The next room in the confusing castle is more like the foyer I entered off the street.

I stand in a sunlit solarium, encased in tempered glass and humid like a greenhouse. Exotic plants flourish in the heat, planted in ornate pots and ancient vases. Weathered historical documents are mounted in museum-like glass boxes around the walls. One of them appears to be the Declaration of Independence, but I assume that it is a replica and continue moving.

Movement at the back of the solarium catches my eye. I crouch low behind a marble bench and peer over a bright yellow flower the size of my head. It is a man, rapidly pacing the floor and talking loudly into a small object I assume to be a phone. No cords trail behind the man but his speech, punctuated by occasional pauses and hesitation, implies that someone else is speaking to him. A quick scan of the room tells me that I am the only other person in the solarium, besides my dead mom, of course.

Ancient and worn stone statues of Greek Gods stand watch over the humid room of flowers. The man continues to move, shouting into the device held to his ear. He walks behind a statue of Poseidon and disappears through a door that I hadn't noticed before.

My mom walks past me, heading directly for the door at the back of the solarium. I reach out as she passes me and touch her hand, making her turn. "Why?" I ask her, indicating the door with my head. She doesn't respond, but pulls away from me and continues toward the door. "Why must I keep going? I don't even know what this place is!" The dead woman stares through the bloody burlap at my crouching form and I can feel her animosity. Her anger seethes and she lowers her shoulders like a great cat getting ready to devour its prey.

I jump to my feet and scramble over the marble bench, heading further into the dense maze of exotic vegetation. Looking over my shoulder, I can see my mom running to catch me with her arms spread wide. Her fingers transform into the long, hairy legs of a massive spider and all around me, I see demons rising up from the ground.

Dozens of beings identical to the featureless man stalk me from amidst the plant life, slowly pushing branches and verdant fronds out of their way. Everywhere I look, the demons continue to surround me.

I run, beating my legs against the floor as fast as they will move.

"I won't follow you!" I yell into the air. The demons stare at me from all around and I know that I cannot move quickly enough to avoid them. "No!" I scream, more frustrated than I have ever been in my life. Determination overwhelms me and all I can think of is victory. Victory here means escape, overcoming the demons and pressing onward, getting myself out of this house and breaking free from the feeling of being herded.

I knock over a large potted plant with broad, purple leaves and it takes a small sculpture down with it. The carved marble shatters on the floor and the demon nearest to me hesitates. I glare at it, taunting it with my confident posture. Another featureless demon approaches from my back and I take off, charging down a tight pathway choked by overgrown ferns.

A statue of a woman without arms stands at the end of the short pathway and I barrel into it, slamming my entire weight into the base of the statue. It rocks back and forth, precariously balancing along its marble edges, and one final push sends it to the ground where it explodes.

Demons shriek and a chorus of painful voices fills the air. The ones that I can see stop moving and stand, staring at me and turning their heads side to side. One of them takes a slow step backward and slinks its shoulders as if in submission.

I run at the demon, spreading my arms out wide and flailing my fists in an attempt to scare the unholy spawn. Something about my crazed appearance strike fear into the creature and it turns, running away from me on all fours. I howl with laughter, showing the demons that I am far more insane than they will ever hope to be.

Running from statue to statue, I trample the exotic plants and turn the priceless antiques into worthless rubble. Turning back to the door I used to enter the room, I spot a strange tree with low hanging branches near the framed Declaration of Independence. I leap from the back of a marble bench and sail through the air with my hand balled into a fist. The glass protecting the document reverberates loudly as it collides with my fist, sending shock waves through it and splintering the wooden frame. I jump up at it again and am able to wrap my fingers around the edges of the frame and rip it from the wall. I fall backward, tossing the heavy object over my head as I land.

A smile creeps onto my face when I hear the frame break apart. The demons scream louder and louder with eerie voices that sound hollow and tormented. Running to the broken frame, I step on the glass as hard as I can and feel the satisfying crunch of it under my shoe as it splinters into hundreds of pieces. I pick up the largest shard of glass and run my finger along the edge. A thick line of blood smears across the sharp point and a dull, throbbing pain emanates from the wound.

"Yes," I hiss more than say. I have a weapon. I look down at the rest of the broken frame and realize that it was my shoe, not my naked foot, that broke through the glass. I am clothed. For the first time since I was pulled through the Johnson's table by the featureless man, I am fully clothed.

Triumphantly, I pump my fist into the air and look for the nearest foe. A featureless demon cowers behind a luscious plant with thick, triangular stalks. Slashing at the plant, I cut a path through the foliage. The shadowy beast looks up at me, tilting its eyeless face in my direction. It screams, bellowing a mighty roar meant to frighten me away. Shadows dance in the back of my vision and chaotic images rush through my mind at a dizzying pace.

None of it is real, I tell myself. I know that I can overcome the demon and my mental resolve pushes the terrifying vision from my consciousness. I bring the broken piece of glass down in front of me in a brutal overhand chop the skewers the naked creature. Laughing, I hack at its neck again, eager to tear the vile beings head from its shoulders. Another mighty cleave has the monster's head rolling away into the foliage with a messy spray of chunky, black blood. I kick the demon's torso and watch it fall to the ground in a pool of its own fluids.

"Nothing can stop me!" I yell at the top of my lungs. The air is warm and the sun shines down on my face like the celestial rays of a holy blessing. All at once, the demons spring to life and attack.

"Stop!" I can hear my mom's strained voice calling from somewhere in the distant corners of the room. "Stop this now, Fletcher Lee! You cannot fight them! You must follow me, for that is the path that has already been set out for you! You cannot break the plan!" Her words are hurried, slurring together in a frantic pace full of fear and uncertainty.

"I will kill!" I shout back at her, not sure of what, exactly, I intend to kill. "Everything!" I settle on, smiling with fire in my eyes. "I will kill everything!" The exclamation feels right on my tongue, like I was born for this one task.

The demons scamper through the solarium, running like dogs for my feet. I slash out with the makeshift dagger, cutting flesh and spinning rapid circles to keep them all at bay. "Be gone!" I yell as a bloodied demon falls in pieces to the ground in front of me. I am fully consumed by the adrenaline rush of battle. Scores of demons press in from every angle but the weapon in my hands kills them as quickly as they come on.

Never have I felt so alive.

Blood runs freely down my arms, staining my shirt sleeves and mixing with the demonic blood to form a layer of thick, coagulated sludge that makes the glass stick to my fingers. I am thankful for the ooze covering my hands and I plunge the deadly glass shard deep into the stomach of the featureless man, letting the demonic blood wash over my body.

The ranks of monsters thin, allowing me passage back to the room full of chained copies of my mother. I burst through the door and ready the glass shard in front of me, anticipating a charge. It doesn't take long to realize that all of the bodies are dead and still, reeking in the cold air. I walk past them without much incident and only look over my shoulder once to make sure I am not followed.

When I reach the large wooden double doors, I push hard against them, expecting them to be locked. The doors swing quietly open, revealing the opulent foyer. Everything in the room is silent except for the soft whirling of the industrial fans mounted to the ceiling of the concrete room at my back.

The mahogany railing banister is cool to the touch and the marble steps squeak gently under my blood-soaked shoes. I grip the glass shard tighter, feeling its edges digging into my hand, and stab the nearest oil painting. The glass shreds the canvas easily, tearing my own face from the picture. I cut myself out of the portrait and move down to the golden fountain, cutting every painting I pass. It takes time and by the end, I am exhausted.

The water in the fountain tastes slightly sweet, like crisp spring water mixed with a few drops of honey. I drink deeply from the fountain, letting the cool water splash over my face and take the blood from my arms. The glass shard falls from my hand and clatters to the floor beside my outstretched legs. With my back against the golden fountain, I hang my head and submit my body to sleep.

Sunday, November 14th, 1976

The Society for the Theological Exploration of the Unknown gathers once again in the undercroft of Saint Timothy's Episcopalian Church. All fourteen members are present, seated before a small wooden table. Pastor Santiago and Doctor Kendrick stand behind the table, ready to address the meeting.

"Thank you all for coming on such short notice," Doctor Kendrick begins. She is dressed unremarkably and feels uncomfortable under the heavy weight of the men's stares. Nervously, she pulls the edges of her jacket in closer over her chest. Most of the society members wore conservative business suits although some of them sport bowler hats and polished canes that are clearly for show. The Money, clearly the youngest member of the society, sits in the front row clad in an outlandish gold leisure suit with buttons made of pearls. He notices Doctor Kendrick's glance and tips the edge of his tall black top hat, flashing a sly smile at just the right moment to make the woman blush.

"As we agreed upon during our last meeting," Pastor Santiago takes over, "we need to figure out a safe way to release Fletcher Lee from wherever the demon took him."

"We aren't even sure where he is!" the professor exclaims to clamoring from the other members. "What if he is in Hell?"

The thought of Fletcher being tormented for eternity makes Doctor Kendrick's voice stick in her throat. "He didn't die," she whispers, barely loud enough for Pastor Santiago to hear.

"Doctor Kendrick has a good insight," the robed pastor tells the gathered men. "If Fletcher went through the portal kicking and screaming, as in alive, he could not have been taken to Hell. Only the souls of the dead can be damned to eternal punishment. Fletcher is somewhere else."

"What have you found in your research?" One of the older

members of the society asks from his seat near the back of the group.

The professor stands to address the society, brushing off his tweed jacket and pulling some documents from his leather briefcase. "You're right. The boy can't be in Hell unless his mortal body has died, and according to everything I have been able to learn in such a short time, his physical being *cannot* die in any of the lower planes."

"How many lower planes are there?" Doctor Kendrick asks.

"No one can be sure of that. We know of Hell, of course, the lowest plane. Other planes commonly known to philosophers and theologians include Tartarus, the plane of fallen angels, and Gehenna, the plane of fallen humans," the professor tells her.

"Don't forget Tzoah Rotachat," The Money chimes in. "That is one of the presumed planes of torment we know of from Jewish history."

"Yes, and we cannot forget Hades, the plane of imprisoned souls that Jesus visited after his death," Pastor Santiago adds. "And Sheol, the plane mentioned in the Old Testament, is known as the land of shades, where lost souls go to wander until Judgment Day."

"Which one of the planes has Fletcher been taken to?" Lissa asks with a voice full of sorrow.

"My guess," the professor explains to her and the rest of the gathered members of the society, "is that if Fletcher was taken by a demon, he must have been taken to Gehenna."

"It should also be noted that in Jewish, Islamic, and Christian texts, Gehenna is known for the torment of children. The word comes from the Valley of Hinnom, an area to the east of ancient Jerusalem where the Babylonian worshippers of Moloch would take their children to sacrifice them in fire. The land was cursed, according to the prophet Jeremiah, and now exists as The Valley of Slaughter." A shudder runs the length of Doctor Kendrick's spine and she thanks Pastor Santiago for taking the time to explain it to her. All of the men in the room nodded throughout the explanation, showing their immense knowledge.

"I say we go down to Gehenna and show those demons that they can't have one of ours!" The Money shouts with visible excitement. Surprisingly, the members of the society begin to voice their agreement.

"Do we just perform the ritual from the book and hope that a portal opens?" Doctor Kendrick questions the pastor.

"Unless anyone has any better ideas, I say we go for it." There is a long pause that fills the undercroft with tension. Pastor Santiago looks around the room, waiting for someone to break the silence.

"Who wants to go?" He finally says. "We will need a couple volunteers."

The Money jumps up, eagerly putting his hand in the air and showing a big smile. "I've been waiting for someone to ask that question!" He shouts just a little too loudly.

"Perfect. Anyone else?" Pastor Santiago stares at the professor until the old man finally raises his hand. "I was hoping you would agree to come along," he tells him.

"I'll go," one of the quieter members of the society says from the back of the room. He is a middle-aged man wearing fine three-piece suit and black bowler hat.

"Who is that?" Doctor Kendrick murmurs. "He hasn't spoken anything yet."

"Ah, Mr. Gronhagen, I am pleased that you will be joining us," Pastor Santiago says with a smile.

The man stands and puts his hands on his waist, revealing a thin golden chain going from one of his vest buttons to his right pocket. "It will be my pleasure, pastor." He tips his hat, "and to tell you the truth, I had the pleasure of meeting your father, Doctor Kendrick, when you were just a young girl. You don't remember me, do you, Lissa?"

Doctor Kendrick scrutinizes the man intensely, searching her memories for his face. She can't place him. "I'm sorry, Mr. Gronhagen, I don't remember you. How did you know my father?"

"Please, call me Anders," he says with another charming smile. "I met Baltasar Kendricksson at a conference in Stockholm back in 1954, we were both there for a week long lecture series on constellations and their meaning throughout history. Baltasar was the keynote speaker; I remember him vividly." His voice is light and airy, similar in tone to Lissa's, and with just enough hint of an accent to be considered exotic.

"Anders works at the observatory and teaches classes in physics and astronomy at the university," Pastor Santiago explains, although Lissa is too busy being astonished to hear him.

"You'll have to forgive me, Anders," Doctor Kendrick says

curtly. "Since I moved to the United States and changed my last name, I have had very little to do with my former life. As I am sure you are aware, my father died in 1961 in his cabin outside of Kiruna. That was the last time I have been back to Sweden."

Anders hangs his head reverently. "Truly, I did not know. It saddens my heart to hear of his passing. I am sure that the scientific community is still reeling from his death. If I may ask, how did he die?"

"No," Lissa says, turning her back to hide her tears. "You may not ask about him. Thank you."

Anders lets out a long sigh and moves forward to place a comforting hand on Lissa's back. "When I met him, he was young, and so full of life that I thought he would never die. Please, Lissa, accept my apology for prying. I am very sorry for your loss."

Doctor Kendrick brushes his hand away moves a step from the table before turning to face Anders. Her eyes are moist and their edges turn rapidly to pink. She sniffs back a sob and reaches a hand out to Anders as a peace offering. He takes it warmly in both hands but doesn't speak another word.

"If everyone is ready and awkward introductions are finished," The Money interrupts, "I would like to get this started. Are we good to head down to the altar?" He looks at Pastor Santiago for permission and the robed man nods his head. The professor stays behind as the other members of the society file out of the undercroft and leave the makeshift team in peace.

"Well," Pastor Santiago says with an outstretched arm pointing to the stairs. "Shall we?"

Gehenna: a place without time.

I awaken with my head still resting against the golden fountain, but everything else has changed. Everything around me lies in ruins. The fountain is dry and rusted and the back half of it looks as though it was hit by a bomb. The curving marble staircase and the gilded walls are nothing but a heap of debris.

My mother stands in front of me, wearing the bloody burlap sack still tightly tied around her neck. She looks down on me, shaking her head within the bag. Her hands are on her hips, a stance I know well from growing up. Her pose is judgmental, scorning, and I feel like hiding under the weight of her stare.

Standing on my feet, I scan the ruined castle for what dangers may be lurking. The sky is dark, an oily grey like the foreboding remnants of an afternoon thunderstorm. Lightning flashes far in the distance and the air smells warm and moist with rain. Vines curl around the fallen chunks of walls and stairs, and abundant plant life reaches up from the soil.

The street outside of the ruined castle, where I watched from the inside as my own house burned around me, no longer exists. A forest, dense with tall trees, surrounds the ruins. The world feels open and massive, like all that I can see before me is less than a speck of the earth. My mother straightens and turns her back on me, walking into the dark forest without looking back.

I take a couple hesitant steps toward the tree line. The ground is moist and my shoes stick in the soft mud. Everything is so different from when I fell asleep that it makes my mind spin. I let the fresh air fill my lungs and try to clear my head before moving any farther from the castle wreckage.

Remembering the weapon, I search near the fountain for the broken shard of glass to take with me but it isn't there. Digging through some of the broken rubble, I am able to find a small length of splintered wood that could possibly be useful as a dagger, but it crumbles in my hands. Everything is rotted. The wood is wet and moldy and I know that it has been buried in the dirt for decades.

I follow my mom's footsteps into the forest and see a well-beaten dirt path winding its way through the thick trees. Animal footprints are scattered along the edges of the trail but the wet ground reveals hundreds of boot impressions. Many people have crossed here by this path and I attempt to muffle my steps in case they are still nearby.

With hurried footsteps, I catch up to my mom and follow behind her, matching her pace but not walking at her side. I hate the feeling of being controlled, but I am thankful there isn't a whip cracking against my back.

We walk down the path for hours, trudging along in silence. The sky never loses its ominous grey tone despite the amount of time that passes during the walk. My mom finally stops walking and stands at the edge of a small ravine. Overgrown remnants of small wooden bridge are scattered among the rocks and flowing water. She stands there, looking down at the stream, and then gazes back at me through the bloody burlap.

A wooden mill is built on the opposite bank of the ravine and the wheel turns slowly. It creaks and squeals as it turns but shows no signs of disuse. My mom points at the building, indicating with her head that I am to go there. "Why?" I ask her, resisting the urge to grab her by the shoulders and throw her to the rocks below.

The front of the burlap moves slightly, as though her mouth is moving, but she doesn't respond. "Why should I listen to you?" I shout in her face. She continues to point and all I can think about is resisting her desires. I don't want to be controlled by anything, even if that means denying my dead mother her wishes.

"Why am I here?" I scream. My frustration boils over and I pound my fists into her chest. She takes a step back and makes no attempt to block my blows or calm me down. "What are you doing to me?" I continue to yell. I pull my fist back and slug her as hard as I can in the stomach. She stumbles, reaching out a hand to catch herself on my shirt. I jerk away from the hand and kick out, landing my foot squarely on the top of her knee. A sound like the snapping of wet twigs accompanies the connection of my shoe and her leg.

I lash out again, hitting her twice in the head, and she crumbles backward on the edge of the ravine. Another kick to her kneecap and she falls. Her head twists, locking my eyes with her bloody burlap, and she plummets over the edge. The drop isn't far, less than twenty feet, but the sharp, jagged rocks waiting at the bottom tear her body apart. A smile spreads over my face as I watch the last twitches of life leave her broken corpse.

Giving her no more thought, I take a few running steps and leap the small ravine, landing painfully on a tree root that bashes my gut and knocks the air from my lungs. I pull myself up and lean against the tree to regain my composure.

The mill continues to creak in the steady current of the small stream and my first thought is to go towards it and investigate. Looking back at the shattered body of my dead mom lying face down in the mud, I know that is what she wanted me to do. I spit into the ravine and resolve to be free of her demands. If the world around me is going to try to force me into certain paths of action, I will do everything in my power to resist, to fight back, to be autonomous.

An oil lamp flickers next to the door of the mill and a rusted out weathervane rocks idly back and forth atop the roof. Multiple voices chatter idly behind the thick, foggy windows. There is a sign hanging from a post by the trail but it is written in a language I don't recognize.

In the soft, fresh mud, the wooden sign pulls free of the ground with ease. I creep up to the door of the mill and slide the sign post through the iron ring set into the banded wood. The sign post is long enough to fit across the entire doorway, effectively preventing the door from being opened.

It doesn't take much searching around the mill to find a stack of firewood tucked away neatly under a woven bough of pine branches. The split logs are rough in my hands and give off a rich aroma of earthly scents that fill my nostrils. After half an hour of work, the logs are piled all around the base of the mill.

The oil lamp hangs from a wrought iron hook mounted just beyond the reach of my fingertips. For a moment, I consider leaving, but a long branch catches my eye and I use it to easily retrieve the lamp.

The thatched roof hangs over the corner of the mill by a few feet, not far from a small square window. I throw the metal lamp fiercely into the corner of the wooden mill and it explodes into a shower of liquid flames.

Fire laps up against the wooden logs and comes to life. The oil spreads the flames quickly, and within moments, the roof catches fire and pushes a great plume of black smoke into the dull sky. The voices inside the mill begin screaming and someone pounds on the door. They try to wrench it open, but the sign post holds and doesn't give the door an inch. Their voices are frantically screaming against the smoke.

I relish the terror, confident that the featureless man who brought me here does not want me to rebel so violently. I think back to my mother's broken body in the ravine and smile; I won't be a slave to the forces that hold me in this personal hell.

A burning figure emerges from a window on the side of the mill, shattering the glass with a fist. The opening isn't large, maybe less than two feet on each side, but the person struggling to fit through is determined. I run to that side of the mill and climb atop some of the unlit logs and push the burning person back into the house. I step back, feeling the heat against my face, and watch the inferno devour the mill. The person screams and makes another attempt at the broken window but I only watch her struggle. I know that the flames and smoke will end her life long before she can manage to crawl through the narrow gap.

I sit down on the edge of the trail and watch as the mill is reduced to ash. Memories of my own burning house fill my head and I think back to my dad, writhing in pain on the floor. I don't know why I am here, or where 'here' is, but my confidence grows with the flames. I can overcome this place, no matter the cost.

After the fires die down and the ruins of the mill are cool enough to sort through, I take one of the unused logs and search for something sufficient to use as a weapon. I miss the feel of the glass shard digging into my palm and slicing through the ranks of featureless demons. The iron banding from the mill's front door sticks up from the smoking rubble and looks heavy enough to cave in a demon's skull. The metal is too hot to touch so I dig it out with the log and let it cool in a soggy patch of mud.

Sitting with my back against a mossy tree trunk, I stare up at the dull grey sky and wonder if the passage of time exists here. It has been hours since I knocked my mom into the ravine and still, the sky has remained the same. No sign of the sun is anywhere to be seen.

Hoof beats spark my attention and I grab the piece of iron banding and crawl further into the forest. The thundering grows louder until finally, from the direction opposite of where I came from, six riders round a bend in the path and approach.

The men are dressed like pictures I've seen in history books about the Middle Ages. Two of them are clad in heavy plates of steel armor that clink loudly with every trot of their horses. They have swords strapped to their hips and their horses are similarly armored and barded with bright colors.

The six horsemen pull on their reins and gather around the ruins of the mill. The one most flamboyantly clothed, who I assume is their leader, raises a gloved fist in the air and dismounts. "Have there been any reports of Norman forces in the area?" he barks with a heavy British accent that I can barely understand. He pushes some of the ashes around with his leather boot.

"Not to my knowledge, sir," one of the other men responds. The speaker dismounts and retrieves a tightly rolled scroll from a pocket inside his blue tunic. "This mill belonged to a man by the name of Rainecourt, sir," he reads from the parchment.

The leader nods and points to the two men at the back of the group. "Fan out and search the area for evidence. If the Normans are here, we need to know." My heart leaps up in my throat and I try to keep my breathing calm to remain hidden. The two men designated to explore begin to spread out and one of them walks in my direction.

I fade back, going deeper into the woods, and try to muffle my footsteps as best I can while maintaining a quick retreat. The man doesn't notice me and the two scouts turn for the direction of the ravine. Thinking on my feet, I decide to follow them and watch from a safe distance.

The men continue on either side of the dirt trail until they reach the collapsed bridge. "If it is the Normans, they couldn't have brought many men with them," one of them says. His accent is harsh and makes him sound uneducated.

"Take a look at this," the other man calls out, pointing to the corpse at the bottom of the ravine. The two men stand on the edge and peer to the water below. "What do you make of that?"

"Normans?" One of them ponders, rubbing his bearded chin. "It looks like a woman . . ."

"Look at the bag on her head; appears she was hung and then tossed in here, you reckon?" The man leans out over the edge and I make my move.

"I don't think—" one of them says as I lunge, swinging the heavy piece of iron in my hands. It connects solidly with the man's back and he tumbles over the edge of the narrow ravine to the waters below. I can hear him moaning and calling out in pain but the one remaining man spins and draws a dagger from his belt.

He opens his mouth to speak and I waste no time. I throw the heavy piece of metal at his chest and follow it with my body, charging in with fists flying. My ferocity takes him by surprise and he drops the dagger. His arms come up in front of his chest to defend himself but he is standing too close to the edge and I hold every advantage. A swift jab with my knee into his groin makes him double over in pain. My elbow collides with the top of his head and I get a hand on his shoulder to send him quickly tumbling after his comrade.

He lands with a sickening thud and I know that he is dead. The bloody gore causes the other man at the bottom of the ravine to resume his shrieking and I know that I have to silence him. I lean over the edge and place a finger over my mouth, but the man ignores my signal. I snatch the dagger from the ground and slide it into the side of my waistband and hold the heavy piece of iron banding high over my head.

The drop isn't terribly far and by dangling my legs over the edge, I am able to make a controlled slide and land safely among the rocks below.

"Please," the survivor begs, "Don't kill me! Have mercy!" The coward's pleading is pathetic. I draw the dagger with my right hand and look at him feebly trying to back away. His left leg is a bloody mess of torn skin and jagged bone. I step on the bottom of the leg and feel the bones of his ankle give way under the pressure.

The man continues to beg for mercy but his words instantly turn to incoherent babbling when I twist my heel into his bone. I drop to my knees and crush my forearm into the coward's nose, snapping his head back against the rocks. "Please . . ." he sobs through a mouthful of dark blood. "My family . . ."

"I will not be controlled," I say in an even tone devoid of remorse. "I will win." The sharp blade of the dagger slides easily under the man's beard. I watch the life leave his eyes. "I told you," I say to the dead man as I wipe the blade off on his tunic, "I will win."

The sound of footsteps heading my way makes me run. I return the dagger to my side and leave the chunk of iron in the stream as I take off. There isn't much room between the edge of the water and the natural dirt wall of the ravine so I have to be careful with my steps. Dodging between boulders and deeper sections of running water, I put the voices behind me and sprint as quickly as I dare.

I pass through a sharp bend in the ravine and stop to catch my breath. I can hear the voices but none of them are giving chase. With the dagger secured firmly in the waistline of my shorts, I walk down the side of the stream until I find an area of the bank suitable to ascend.

I come up near a village, presumably the one that dispatched the riders, and find a stable to hide inside until I can formulate a plan. The village is small, with only a dozen or so buildings. In the center of the quaint town stands a large, rectangular church with a steeple reaching into the sky.

Sitting among the smelly hay and surrounded by horses, I can't help but smile. The demons want to devour me, to destroy me, but I will not follow their plan. My fate is my own and now that I have a reliable weapon, I cannot be stopped. The devil himself will have to take my soul if he wants it so badly.

Sunday, November 14th, 1976

Doctor Kendrick stands behind the four men in the cramped, dark quarters of the room underneath Saint Timothy's Episcopal Church. She reaches into her pocket and takes comfort in the cool feel of the metal crucifix. The small religious icon gives her strength and wards off some of the panic that threatens to consume her life.

"What do we do?" The Money asks tentatively. The others look around the room and it is clear that no one has a good answer.

"The book says that we need to have a demon present," Pastor Santiago says. He glances nervously around the room's shadows as though searching for a demonic presence. "Do you have any ideas how to confirm or deny the presence of demons, Mr. Fitzpatrick?"

Doctor Kendrick smiles and mouths the name silently to herself, thankful to have something other than 'professor' to call the older man.

"Sadly, I do not know. I have never, to my knowledge, been in the presence of a true demon. Perhaps we could attempt to use the book and summon one?" Mr. Fitzpatrick rubs a hand over his chin and stares into the fragrant ooze that coats the altar.

The Money reaches his hand down to the black substance and draws the Latin phrase 'de profundis' with a finger. "Did Fletcher's neighbor say anything else about the moment he was taken?"

Doctor Kendrick shakes her head. "No, she just said the boy uttered that phrase and then was pulled through the table." She turns to the pastor to look for answers. "The book says we need darkness and an innocent person of faith, right?"

The holy man places a hand on her shoulder as he speaks. "Yes, and I am not sure that an innocent person has ever been inside this room, now or otherwise."

"What do you mean?" she asks.

"What the good pastor is saying," the Swede explains, "is that no one is innocent. Not even a child. The only innocent man to have walked our plane died on a cross almost two thousand years ago."

The room falls silent. Confused expressions look to one another for guidance but there is none to be found. After a long moment passes, an idea strikes the only woman of the group.

"I know where we can find a demon, at least," she says excitedly. "Fletcher told me that the featureless demon he sees often lurks around his father's car."

The Money laughs and claps his hands. "Well then why are we down here in the dark? I want to see this demon for myself." He moves toward the door and stands there, waiting for the others to follow.

"I see no reason to remain here if we have the location of a known demon easily within reach." Pastor Santiago ushers the group from the bottom of the church and to the parking lot.

"Well, what do you know?" Doctor Kendrick gasps when the group emerges onto the dimly lit blacktop.

"Mr. Lee!" Pastor Santiago exclaims. "What brings you to church at such a late hour?" His orange and black AMC Javelin is parked under a hazy streetlight.

Rich Lee looks at the group for a moment before settling his gaze firmly on Doctor Kendrick. "What are you doing here?" He demands.

"Mr. Lee, please, I . . ." she stammers, "*we* were just meeting here and discussing some religious alternatives for medicine at the hospital." The lie tastes foul on her tongue but she fears the truth would scare the man away.

"Alright," Rich murmurs, unconvinced but willing to accept the answer. His eyes linger on the psychologist for a moment before returning to Pastor Santiago. "I would like to speak with you, if you have any time," he says. His voice sounds sad and defeated, without any of the bluster it once had.

Pastor Santiago looks to the others and sighs. "Go on without me," he whispers. "You'll do just fine, I have no doubt." He greets Rich with an outstretched hand and leads him back into the church with a smile.

"Ask and ye shall receive," The Money jests. He jogs to the car and runs a finger across the beautiful paint. "So, where is this demon?"

"Trust me, Montesquieu, if you ever see a demon, you will not be laughing," Fitzpatrick reminds him solemnly. "Don't get distracted." The professor bends over and peers into the car's window.

Doctor Kendrick stands a few paces from the car and stares at it, wondering how something as mundane as a vehicle could possibly harbor the evil of a demon.

Anders walks up next to her and lets out a long sigh. "I never imagined that it would be under circumstances such as these that I would meet you again, Lissa," he says.

Lissa shoots him a side-long look and steps away, moving closer to the Javelin. The streetlight flickers overhead and a jolting movement in the corner of her vision catches the woman's attention. She whirls, pointing into the darkness. "I saw something," she tells the other three members of the group.

"A demon?" The Money asks with excitement. He looks past Doctor Kendrick's pointing finger and starts to rush into the darkness before another flicker of the streetlight causes him to retreat.

"I think," Mr. Fitzpatrick says and clears his throat, "that the hour is upon us. Gather round now." He pulls a small jar from his briefcase and sets it down on the back of the Javelin. It is full of the sweet smelling black ooze which he liberally applies to the trunk with two of his fingers.

The light continues to flicker, becoming more of a strobe light than a consistent source of illumination. A great, howling wind picks up and the air pressure noticeably drops. "You are right, Lissa," Anders says as he joins the others at the back of the car. "There must be a demon here."

Tiny beads of hail begin to rain down upon the parking lot and the wind intensifies. The light continues to flicker and produces a sharp, high-pitched buzzing sound as though the bulb is on the verge of explosion.

"Oh, just go out already!" Lissa screams through the torrent of wind and hail. She kicks the base of the light post and the thing burns brighter, throwing a wide arc of light around the Javelin. Lissa looks around frantically and realizes that the streetlight above her head is the only source of light holding the darkness at bay. The church is so dark that she cannot make out the steeple. Other streetlights were shining when she entered the parking lot, but now they are all cold and black.

With a shout of frustration that is immediately lost in the wind, Doctor Kendrick kicks the post one more time and the world around her vanishes. All she can see is the oily blackness of a world devoid of light. The hail stops, along with the wind, and everything is as silent as it is dark. She takes a breathless step forward, reaching out to the car, and latches onto the cold metal under her fingers.

"Be ready," she hears from the darkness to her left. The Money's hand clamps down tightly over her own and for a brief moment, she is thankful.

"From the depths, I have cried out to you, O Lord!" The professor yells.

A whisper creeps into the back of Lissa's mind. It is a voice not generated of her consciousness, but something altogether foreign. *Again,* it urges with a sinister voice.

"From the depths, I have cried out to you, O Lord!" The professor repeats, shouting the line louder.

*Yes, yes, I like that,* the subtle whisper cackles. *One more time, please, darling, just one more time.* Doctor Kendrick digs her fingers into The Money and screams, trying to force the voice from her head.

"From the depths, I have cried out to you, O Lord!" An unholy chorus of laughter fills the night and drowns out all else.

As one, thousands of demonic voices chant a twisted version of the psalm, mocking the righteous efforts of the professor. "We have heard your voice," they say with unhallowed glee. "Our ears are attentive, but your supplication only marks your iniquities ever clearer!" The shadows thicken around Lissa's vision and she slaps at her face, thinking that something has been tied around her eyes.

The demons continue to howl with pleasure from every angle. "Who shall stand?" They taunt with a thousand voices. "Who shall stand? Who shall stand?"

A soft, overwhelmingly evil presence squirms in Doctor Kendrick's mind. It skitters, crossing over the barriers of her subconscious and wrenching horrid images to the front of her brain. She pounds a fist into her temple and tries to shake the otherworldly presence loose, but the demon only laughs.

With one last perversion of scripture, the demon fills her mind with echoing words that shake the foundations of her sanity. *More than watchmen wait for the dawn.*

*More than watchmen wait for the dawn...*

Gehenna: a place without time.

An unknown rustle in the stable disrupts my sleep. I open my eyes but remain still, partially covered in hay. The barn door opens and a middle-aged man walks through holding a pitchfork. I hold my breath and try to pull myself further under the hay without making any noise. The man walks closer, pitching large piles of hay from one area of the stable to another. A horse whinnies and startles me, nearly making me jump.

The man walks over to the horse and pats it firmly on the neck. The great creature nuzzles his arm playfully and bites at the man's skin. He drops the pitchfork and feigns injury, yelling at the horse all the while.

Watching the two beings bond, I smile, and forget where I am. I miss my dog, Corson, and I want more than anything to run up to the horse and touch its mane.

"What's his name?" I ask, lifting my head from the hay for an instant. As soon as I speak, I remember where I am and panic. The man looks at me and freezes. For one breath, time stands still.

I explode into motion, leaping into the air and running for the door as fast as I can. The dagger is still tucked away in my shorts and I consider drawing it, but the long pitchfork at the man's feet is too much for me to defend against. I run past him, ignoring his shouts, and bolt through the door.

Thankfully, the farmer is content with yelling at my back as I fade away into the woods surrounding the village.

I hate being an outcast and living in the woods, but I see no way to join them after what I did to the mill. Although it is morning and I can taste dew on the misty air, the sky still gives off a dull grey pallor like an afternoon storm.

Standing behind a mossy tree that affords me a clear view of the village center, I watch the farmer rallying the other villagers around him. A dozen or so grimy looking peasants listen to the farmer and watch as he points in my general direction. I look behind me and map out a mental route of escape should they gather torches and pursue me like a medieval monster.

An armored soldier steps out from the church and calms them down with a wave of his hand. He wears a plumed helmet emblazoned with a blue lion and golden epaulets on his shoulders.

I sneak closer to the village to try and hear what the soldier is saying. "Normans have not been sighted in the area!" he shouts through a thick English accent. The peasants clamor at the proclamation, pointing into the woods and yelling.

"A witch!" one of the commoners yells at the top of her lungs. The crowd immediately takes up the chant and despite the calming measures of the soldier, the rabble continues to riot. After a few minutes of the soldier trying to quiet them, he finally throws his hands up and walks back into the church alone.

The crowd continues to shout about witchcraft and heresy until they disperse back into their houses a long time later. One of the villagers, the haggard old woman who started the shouting about witchcraft, stays in the center of the buildings and slumps against a ditch on the side of the road. I watch her, curious as to why she does not return to the hovel she came from.

Every villager that happens to walk by her gets a stern tongue lashing about witchcraft and devil worship. "The town loony," I murmur under my breath. "The woman is nuts."

"A witch is what killed them Rainecourts at the mill!" she yells at a little boy who cases a squirrel through the streets. A woman carrying a sloshing pail of water toward to the church stops for a brief moment and listens to the old hag rant. "For years I've been saying that witch Martha is the one been killing everyone 'round here. No damned Normans…" She points a ragged finger at a small stone cottage near the barn I was hiding in and yells the supposed witches name again.

"A witch," I realize aloud. "Maybe a witch could help me." I wander in the direction of the grubby woman's pointing finger and sneak below a small square window. The cottage is tiny, but has multiple wooden trapdoors leading to the cellar.

I test the trapdoors one by one until I find a handle that opens, revealing a small, rotted ladder that descends into darkness. The first step crumbles into splinters beneath my weight so I grab the trapdoor and jump, landing on my feet and slamming the door shut above my head. Silently, I wait in the utter darkness for a long moment to make sure that no one heard the clang of the door and is coming to investigate.

The underground chamber is small, with rough, wet stones on all sides like the bottom of a well. A few shelves are cut into the walls, but they hold nothing more than a couple of scattered rat nests.

Another door is set into the stone waist high and it easily swings open to reveal another passageway moist with slick slime. A soft flicker of light bounces off the rock and casts a soft glow throughout the tunnel. Without many other options, I drop to my knees and crawl through the space. The tunnel isn't long, only about double the length of my body, and I reach the other end effortlessly.

Smoke drifts up from a wall-mounted torch and stings my lungs. I grip the edge of the tunnel opening and pull my head out to survey the room. A woman, one I assume to be Martha, sits at a tiny rocking chair and dips string into a vat of boiling wax to make candles.

"Martha?" I call to her from across the room. She turns and stares at me with beady eyes so full of cataracts that the only color reflected in them is grey that matches the sky.

"Yes, yes, child, do come in," she sputters, never unlocking my eyes from her blind stare. She motions to me with a wrinkled hand so I pull myself all the way through the tunnel and drop about six feet to the hard dirt floor.

"The boy from the future," she says, eagerly standing and shaking my hand. "I have always wanted to meet you."

"What?" How does she know who I am? Am I actually in the past? A whirlwind of thoughts consumes my mind and I am taken by memories of the child I killed on the war torn streets and the family I burned alive in their mill.

"Don't be alarmed, my child," she chuckles happily as she returns to her rocking chair. Standing next to her seated form, I tower over her and realize that she is a dwarf.

"How do you know me?" I demand, taking a belligerent pose

with my hand on the hilt of my dagger.

"I thought I told you to calm down," she tells me without looking. She dips another string into the wax and lets it sit. Stacks of thick, crinkled paper are scattered about the table in front of her and one of them catches my eye. It is a document similar to a blueprint that is covered in drawings of archery bows from different perspectives.

"What are you?" The woman cackles, holding her belly and laughing while she digs through the stack of papers. Finally, she turns and hands me one. "Nothing is written on this, Martha," I tell her, handing the sheet back.

"Oh, it is always the same with you children from the future. You never learn to look with your eyes." She points to my chest and grimaces. "You only see with your *eyes*." Nothing she says makes any sense to me. I set the blank page down on the cluttered table and shake my head.

"What am I supposed to do?" I want to know.

As though the answer was the most trivial thing in the world, the woman scoffs. "Make arrows, of course!" Her laughter returns and I am left to contemplate the cryptic response without any further explanation. She pulls the string from her small pot of wax and places the candle on a rack to cool.

"Make arrows . . ." I search the depths of my knowledge for some sort of meaning but come up with none. I have never shot an arrow in my life and don't know the first thing about archery. "What would I do with arrows?"

The old dwarf turns back to me and reaches up to tap my forehead forcefully. "That is the question. What *would* you do with arrows, child from the future?"

"My name! You know my name!" I exclaim. "Fletcher, it means someone who makes arrows, right?" The dwarf laughs again, nodding her head and handing me the blank piece of parchment again.

I look back to the paper and see nothing, but fold it and put it in my pocket instead of returning it to her. "Now you are learning," she tells me as she dips another string into the hot wax.

"Help me with these, arrow maker." She hands me a string and demonstrates what I am supposed to do. I grab another stool from the corner of the small room and sit next to her while I dip my candle. "We are going to need a lot of them," she says with a smile.

"For what?" I wonder. I watch the wax congeal around the string as I pull it up and down in the pot.

"You don't know? You can't feel it?" She acts surprised, but I have no idea what she is referring to. "You have many visitors, arrow maker."

We sit in silence for the better part of an hour, making candles and placing them on the wooden rack to cool. The old dwarf hums to herself, but makes no other attempts at explaining anything to me.

Once we have thirty or so candles hanging from the rack, she motions for me to stop. "What do we do now?" I ask her, but she says nothing. Martha moves to another wall and takes a small glass jar from a shelf. She hands it to me and gestures for me to open it as though her withered arms aren't strong enough.

I pry the lid from the jar and hand it to her. A strong, overwhelming aroma fills the room from the open container. It smells sweet, like dark chocolate, and brings forth memories of a vacation I took once with my family to a chocolate factory in Pennsylvania.

Martha pours some of the dark ooze from the jar and smears it around the table. The pungent smell, while ultimately enjoyable, is so strong that it makes my head hurt and I have to take a few steps back. I watch the old dwarf place the candles we made in a circle around the ooze and she lights them with the wall torch.

"Your visitors have been waiting for quite some time, I fear. I hope nothing has happened to them at the door." Martha looks to me with her grey eyes and takes on an air of seriousness. "Shall we open it for them?"

I nervously bring forth the dagger from my shorts and wait. "What's going to happen? Who are these visitors?" The dwarf doesn't say anything but scrawls a line of letters in the ooze and steps back. She covers her ears with her hands and I do the same, closing my eyes tightly in case of an explosion.

A loud pop fills the room and deafens me, despite my efforts at protecting my ears. The shockwave that follows hits me full in the chest like a heavy hammer and I fall backward against the wall, temporarily disoriented.

When I open my eyes, I can't believe what I see. Doctor

Kendrick sits on the dwarf's stool, panting for breath, and thin wisps of smoke trail up from her body as though she came from a raging inferno. "I would move from the stool, if I were you," the dwarf says cheerfully.

I see that the doctor is too stunned to move on her own so I grab her shoulder and jerk her from the stool to the ground just before another loud pop rips through the room like thunder.

Two men, neither of whom I recognize, spill into the room. Their tumbling, smoking bodies turn the stool into splinters. The circle of candles sputters and the dwarf springs into action. She grabs the torch and tries to relight the wicks but the fire doesn't take.

"Blast," she exclaims, visibly exhausted. "There was one more that didn't make it through." She offers a hand to one of the men and lifts him from the floor. All three of the 'visitors' gasp for breath and their clothes smolder with the remnants of a fire. Martha beats a patch of flames from the shoulder of one of the men and turns to me. "Still," she says, "three out of four is a personal best."

"What are you doing here, Doctor Kendrick?" I ask as I rush to her side. She places a weary hand on my shoulder and struggles to regain her sense.

"Fire…" she says to no one in particular. "So much . . . fire." She rubs her wrists and I can see deep red marks indicative of chains.

"What happened to you?" The tall woman collapses to the ground, succumbing to unconsciousness and Martha rolls her to her side. The two men seem to be in similar states of shock although the younger one does his best to stand on his own and clear his head.

"Who are you?" I ask them, grabbing a hat that tumbled to the floor and holding it out to him. Ashes and a layer of white dust coat the expensive looking hat.

"Wilfred Montesquieu, at your service," the man says as he brushes off the hat and returns it to his head. "And this fine gentleman is Anders Gronhagen, a friend of Doctor Kendrick's."

"How did you get here?" I ask, looking more to Martha than anyone else.

"We were looking for you," Anders says. He smiles and points to my chest but his finger wavers from tiredness.

Doctor Kendrick finally opens her eyes and looks around the room with confusion. "Where is the professor, Mr. Fitzpatrick? Why isn't he here yet?"

Martha walks over to her and offers her a comforting hug. "I couldn't get him through, dear," she whispers. Her grave tone betrays the danger that the professor must be experiencing.

"Where is he?" I ask.

"I don't know. I could feel him coming through, knocking on the door, but when I opened it, he didn't walk through. I don't know where he might be." Martha shakes her head and starts putting the candles back on the cooling rack. She uses a small knife to scrape the black ooze from the table back into the jar.

"Could something have held him back? Was it his choice to go through?" Doctor Kendrick is worried for the man's soul.

"Is it ever our choice?" Anders replies. He looks right at me and his blue eyes bore into me with their intensity. "When you came here, Fletcher, did you choose it? I am under the impression that you were kidnapped, more or less."

I think about the question for a long time. Did I choose to come here? The featureless man certainly pulled me through the table, but I read the words that he wrote in the ooze. I was so mad at Mr. Johnson, all I wanted to do was get away from there, wherever that meant. Did some part of me choose to come to this place?

"I'm not even sure what this place is," I say, to blatantly avoid the question. I remember the distinct feeling of conquest and victory I had when I overpowered the boy on the street with a chunk of pavement. I remember the rush of blood and adrenaline I felt when I destroyed the castle at the end of my street. Victory tasted even sweeter when I burned the mill and killed the guards.

Did I choose to come here? Perhaps not, but I have certainly taken pleasure in many of the things I have done.

"Why didn't you ask?" Martha chuckles and punches me softly in the ribs. I stand a head taller than her which makes me feel awkward. I have never looked down on an adult before. "You are in the small village of Pevensey, just west of Hastings, arrow maker."

"I don't even know where that is, either." I admit. Since I was removed from school, I haven't been able to learn much geography.

"England, arrow maker, you are in England." The old dwarf laughs hysterically at my ignorance. "Why do you think everyone rants about the Normans all the time? Where else would you be?"

"I certainly expected something a little more . . ." Anders struggles to find the right words. "Hellish, I suppose."

"Why?" Martha asks with a heavy amount of arrogance lacing her voice. "Is England supposed to be Hell compared to your future? Or did you actually die before I brought you through the door?"

"I'm truly sorry," Anders tells her, "Trust me, we all have very much to learn."

Voices ring out in a series of shouts overhead and heavy footsteps thunder above the ceiling, making dust and dirt fall from the rafters into my eyes. "Best be going," Martha commands quietly. She pushes us toward the small opening that I crawled through and Wilfred grabs a narrow wooden ladder from the corner and props it against the wall.

"Climb," she urges in a whisper. "Get to the woods and run east," she indicates with a finger. "If you go far enough, you will find a fortress built out of stone. The one you seek will be inside the fortress." Anders and Wilfred are halfway through the tunnel. Doctor Kendrick reaches the top of the ladder and looks back, asking with her eyes if I am going to follow. I nod, waving her onward with a hand.

"You," the dwarf grabs my hand as I step up to the ladder. "Make arrows, boy from the future, make arrows for the Son of the Morning." I scramble up the ladder and through the tunnel on my hands and knees. Anders stands on the ground above the cellar door and reaches down to pull Doctor Kendrick up and then myself.

"Thanks," I say, and the four of us take off running into the woods.

*****

The dense forest gives way to a clearing filled with unexpected light that pours from the dull grey sky. A tall stone fortress built in the shape of a square dominates the area. "Did she say who lives there?" Anders asks as we crouch behind a small rise in the dirt and watch the building for movement.

"She told me to make arrows for the Son of the Morning," I recite. "I don't know what that means, but 'Son of the Morning' sounds like a reference to God." I look to the others for help.

Anders shakes his head. "Son of the Morning or Son of the Dawn means Lucifer. In Latin, the word 'Lucifer' directly translates to 'Bearer of Light.' The devil, if the direct Hebrew translations are to be believed, was the Morning Star and the Son of the Dawn before being cast into the pits of the undead."

Wilfred, the one they call The Money, laughs to himself. "I thought the devil was supposed to be all full of darkness and evil, not light. Did I miss something in church for all those years?"

Doctor Kendrick speaks up, drawing everyone's attention. "My father used to talk about the devil being a creature of deception and trickery. It doesn't surprise me that in the original texts of the Bible, Lucifer was the bringer of light. If the devil wants anything from humanity, it would be to deceive us, no matter what. Why wouldn't he work to change his reputation to one of darkness if he really brings light?"

"I'm not sure I follow you, but I believe you," The Money says, voicing my thoughts perfectly.

"I am under the impression that this plane is not Hell. We are in a lower plane, certainly, but without our physical bodies dying on earth, we cannot be condemned, and therefore, cannot be in Hell." Anders sits with his back to a moss-covered tree and loses himself in deep thought.

"If we are not in Hell," Doctor Kendrick wonders, "then who lives in that fortress? It can't be the Son of the Morning, right?"

"It seems like here, I know nothing," I tell her and stand, walking out from the tree line to approach the fortress. "Martha said to make arrows for the Son of the Morning. We aren't going to figure that out by sitting here and wasting time. The answers we need are in there." I point to the stone fortress and the large wooden double doors swing open, as if responding to my command.

"Might as well," The Money murmurs. The four of us walk through the grassy clearing and stop in front of the fortress doors. The building towers above the trees, reaching up to the dreary clouds like a skyscraper. We cross the last green expanse and stand in the massive doorway feeling small and alone.

The interior of the fortress is surprisingly bare. Nothing adorns the walls, not even sconces to hold torches. Light drifts down lazily from the ceiling although its source is so far overhead that I can't see what it is. There are no rooms inside the building, no walls blocking our path or guiding us in a certain direction.

We walk for what feels like an hour, but the fortress was certainly not that large on the outside. Finally, an object ahead breaks the sameness. A tall throne sits on the stone floor, equidistant from the walls on either side. The chair is beautifully decorated, made from a dark wood full of intricate carvings that shimmer in the light. A delicate red cushion sits on the seat of the throne.

Suddenly, a man appears seated on the throne, wearing a charismatic smile and a suit made out of silk, the likes of which I have never seen. His skin is pale, almost milky, and his thinning hair is the color of golden straw. "Hello," he says quietly. The man's voice echoes from the stone walls, giving it an eerie quality and sending shivers down my spine.

"What are you?" The Money demands rudely. He takes a step back and raises his hands. The man doesn't turn his head to respond, but continues to look at me as though I am the only person he can see.

"How are you today, Fletcher?" He asks. The man rotates his wrist to look at a large, silver watch and then smiles. "I hope that my home has been hospitable to you. I would hate to cause you any trouble, Fletcher." His voice is smooth, full of deep notes and melodic tones like a singer.

"I'm alright," I respond. I don't know what to say. I think he is a demon, but he looks so real and so different from the featureless man.

"I'm sorry about that," he tells me. Flashes of the featureless man flicker through my vision and I know beyond a doubt that the man on the throne has read my mind.

"What's your name?" I ask, trying to catch him off guard.

"Helel Ben-Shachar," the man replies calmly. "But I have been called millions of names throughout the histories of your plane." His eyes bore into me and he stands, towering over me and making even Doctor Kendrick look small in his shadow. "I have answered a question for you, Fletcher Lee. Now you must answer a question of mine."

I gulp down my fear and step closer. The man glowers and my courage feels foolish. I want to run or to hide but I know that it would pointless. Martha sent me here for a reason. "What is it?" I try to keep my voice steady and suppress my emotion.

"It is a question that you need to first answer yourself, Fletcher. Then, only when you have answered it in your own heart, return to me and tell me your answer." He points to my pocket and grins. I can feel the paper that Martha gave me burning with energy and know that I need to read. At least, someone wants me to read it.

I draw the dagger from my waist and look down at my pocket. I could easily stab through the fabric and cut the paper without looking at it. The man starts to laugh, subtle at first, but growing louder. The paper feels rough and crinkled in my fingers. It reminds me of something very old that has been soaked through by water and allowed to dry hundreds of times.

The paper is still folded and I move the dagger point closer to the document. I want more than anything to stab it through and shred it without reading it, but the man's laughter worries me.

"Go ahead," he says with glee. "Destroy it. Cut it to ribbons like you stabbed the man in the ravine. You hold the power in your hands, Fletcher. *You* have to make the choice."

I look at him again and try to show determination in my eyes but somehow, I know the man is mocking me. The paper unfolds loudly in my hands. My eyes scan the paper and I see something written, but it is a language I don't understand.

Anders is standing directly behind me and reaches a hand over my shoulder. "Koine Greek," he says confidently, "a fragment of scripture."

"What does it say?" I look to him and see his eyes scanning the document. He nods occasionally, silently mouthing the words to himself as he translates.

"It is from Luke, the tenth chapter," he begins. "And no man knows who the Son is, but the Father; and who the Father is, but the Son, and he to whom the Son will reveal him."

"It sounds like a riddle," I tell Anders. I look to the man standing in front of the throne for clarification, but he is gone. A glance around the room shows me that he is nowhere to be found.

"What does it mean?" Doctor Kendrick asks. I point toward the throne and she gasps. All of them were too focused on the paper to have noticed the man's disappearance.

"What now?" I wonder. "I don't know what I am supposed to do."

The floor beneath my feet rumbles and a spider web of cracks spreads out from the throne. The four of us run backward and stand close together. The stone floor splits open and the throne tumbles into a gaping chasm. A faint orange glow of fire flickers from the depths and beckons to me with a gentle voice hidden behind the crackling flames. *Come,* it whispers, *find your destiny. Find your salvation, Fletcher Lee.*

I take a few tentative steps toward the opening in the stone and return the crinkled paper to my pocket. "Steps," I tell the group. "We are supposed to go down."

"Will that lead to another plane?" The Money asks. No one knows, therefore no one responds. "I guess we have to go down before we can go back up," he says with a hint of frustration.

The stairs are hot, not like the heat from the raging fire that consumed my house, but debilitating like the sticky grip of a humid summer day. The air is hard to breath and my head begins to sweat almost instantly as we descend the stone staircase.

Torches are fastened with iron sconces to the walls every few feet. As far as I can see, the steps continue down for a couple of stories and then level out into an underground passage. We walk for another ten feet and then reach a large wooden door. I wipe the beading sweat from my forehead and push the door open.

The room behind the door is massive, the size of a baseball field at least, with a large bonfire blazing in the center. No hole has been cut into the ceiling to allow the smoke to escape but the chamber is tall enough to accommodate the dark cloud.

"Doors," Doctor Kendrick says, walking to a much smaller opening set into the circular stone wall. A thick layer of old grime and ash coats the face of the door. I slide my fingers across it, clearing a small section of the wood, and reveal etchings. "What it is?" Doctor Kendrick says as she starts to clear the door with her hand.

The four of us scrape the dust from the wood and step back, inspecting the intricate etchings in the low firelight. "It looks like a gun," I think aloud. A revolver has been carved into the wooden door and a small iron ring is set into the wooden planks where the trigger is depicted.

The Money fidgets nervously at my side and takes a step back. "What is it?" I ask him, drawing everyone's attention. He continues to backpedal, clearly unnerved by the etching.

"Is there something you haven't told us?" Anders demands. The older Swede steps in front of The Money and places a hand forcefully on his shoulder.

"I . . ." he stammers. "That's my gun." The Money pulls back the side of his expensive jacket and draws a revolver from a leather holster that hangs from his shoulder. The etching on the door lights up behind me and with a moment of clarity, I know what we are meant to do.

"That door is yours," I tell him calmly. "Open it and go through." I search the rest of the massive underground area and spot what looks like another dust-coated door farther off. "There is a door for each of us down here."

The Money gulps down his fears and grabs the iron ring. With a swift tug, it opens. I can't see anything on the other side, but The Money lifts a hand to his eyes as though a blinding light pours forth from the door. "Go," I command. "We will meet you on the surface."

I don't know what makes me so confident, but somehow I feel a new wave of steadiness washing over my body.

The next door is covered with an even thicker layer of grime and dust but the three of us remove it eagerly. "A constellation," Anders says once we have the door cleared. "Libra, the scales, by the looks of it." He takes a deep breath and reaches for the iron ring. "This one is meant for me." He turns as the door flares with energy and salutes us. "See you on the top . . . Both of you." With a fearless step, he passes through the open door and into a place I cannot see.

"Two more, I bet," I say to Doctor Kendrick. She looks down at me and ruffles my hair, but I can see true fear behind her blue eyes. I know that she is doing everything she can to keep from breaking down and crying. "That fire is so hot," I tell her, trying to keep her mind preoccupied.

We walk around the curve of the wall and come to another door. The grime and soot coating the portal is so thick that a chisel or metal scraper almost necessary. "Finally," I say, tired from clawing at the dirty surface. Doctor Kendrick and I take a step back to examine the door. The carving is old and nearly undetectable in the gentle light.

"This one is mine," she whispers. Her voice quavers and she reaches a hand to the corner of her eye. A winged staff is carved into the door with two snakes wrapping around it.

"The symbol of medicine," I say. "You will be fine." I want to comfort her but I don't know how. She looks down at me and crouches, embracing me in a warm hug. "Thank you," I whisper to her softly.

I can feel her tears smearing the dirt on my cheek. "I will see you again, Fletcher. We will get out of this place." She stands and grabs the iron ring on the door. The etching flares to life and the tall woman steps through, leaving me alone with the fire and the smoke.

It doesn't take long to locate the last door. The stone around the door is covered in a fine, white powder as though the rock was recently cut. The door, showing no signs of age or dust, is blank. I run my fingers over the surface, wondering if there are etchings carved into it that I can't see, and I feel a subtle pulse of energy hit my fingertips.

"Is this one mine?" I ask the darkness. Nothing responds. For an instant, I consider ripping the dagger from my belt and hacking at the door, showing the world my defiance, but the idea is fleeting.

"I don't want to kill any more . . ." I mumble, thinking back on what happened all of the other times I tried to break free of the path laid out before me.

I touch the ring on the door and feel another burst of energy pulling me, urging me to open it. Trying to harden my emotions and summon every ounce of courage present in my body, I pull the door open and close my eyes.

Warm sunlight falls on my face and a swift breeze rushes through my hair. I clench my eyes tightly, not wanting to see what lies ahead, and stumble into the area beyond.

*****

Wilfred Montesquieu grips the handle of his Colt Navy so tightly that his knuckles turn white. "What is this place?" He yells, waving the pistol around in front of him. Hundreds of shriveled, naked children claw at his feet from every direction. The man stands in a village on an open plain, shielding his eyes from the bright rays of sunlight that bake his skin. Grass huts and the occasional ragged tree dot the landscape.

"Get back!" he screams into the face of a child, barely past the age of infancy. The haggard boy pleads with his eyes for mercy, but all The Money sees is a dirty hand about to stain his expensive pant leg.

"I'm warning you!" the man shouts. With delirious intensity, he waves the pistol in front of him and clips one of the children in the side of the head with the long barrel. The naked child recoils and clutches his bleeding scalp, but only for a moment. Hunger overpowers the starving boy and he reaches back to The Money with his hands held in the shape of a cup.

"Filthy beggars!" Wilfred kicks out with his polished shoe and knocks a little girl to the side violently. She attempts to scream but the only voice her small body can make is a pathetic whine more suited to a dying animal than a human being. Her arm reaches out to break her fall, but the girl's wrist is so tiny that it snaps under the pressure and she collapses into a heap of snotty sobs and whimpers. The other children clamor over her and push her aside, trampling her into the ground.

"Vermin! Get back!" The Money yells, pointing his pistol at the nearest of the filthy children and pulling back the hammer. "This is your final warning, I mean it!"

A starving child reaches up and grabs him by the back of his knee, pulling feebly at his leg to turn the man around. The Money whirls on him and fires a shot, purposely missing the boy's head but not by much. The kid, and most of the others nearby, shriek and clutch at their ears. Wilfred nearly loses the pistol from the recoil and the flash creates two large, purple spots in his vision. His ears ring and some of the children fall back, but still others press on.

He tries to run, kicking the beggars aside as he moves, but the sea of children is too thick. One of the huts to his left is open and a man stands next to it using a stack of dollar bills to fan himself. Wilfred calls out to the man for help but receives no reply. "Don't you hear me?" He begs, hitting another child in the skull with the barrel of his pistol. "I need your help man, don't just stand there in the shade!"

A naked boy jumps up from the side of his vision and claws at The Money's face, tearing a thin line of blood down his check. Wilfred turns, batting the child away, and fires a bullet straight through the emaciated boy's ribcage. Blood explodes from his chest and back as he falls to the dusty ground. The child screams, turning their anger into a frenzy, and the mob presses on even harder.

The trigger of the Colt Navy clicks back again and another bullet slices a devastating line through a starving girl's neck, coating the four children behind her in a spray of gore. Two more shots shatter the air and for a moment, a path opens before him. Wilfred darts through the crowd of children and stops next to the other man, panting for breath and holding his hands over his ears.

"It takes a long time for the pain to fade," the man says as he moves the stack of cash back and forth in front of him like a fan. "The ringing, I mean," he clarifies with a smile.

"Who are you?" The Money asks, speaking far too loudly for their close proximity. His eardrums feel like they have ruptured from the gunshots and the only thing he can understand is his own shouting.

The calm man feigns offense and drops the stack of cash to the dusty ground. "You don't know?" he says with mocking surprise. "But Wilfred, just look closer, you know us, don't you?" Something about the confident way the man laughs gives The Money pause. Finally, he realizes that he is looking at a copy of himself.

The clone kicks the stack of cash over to him and chuckles. "Here, give this to the children, see if they can eat money like you do to survive."

Confusion overwhelms Wilfred and nearly brings him to his knees. "What?" he manages to stammer. "Why?"

"All you have done with your life is spend, spend, spend," the clone says judgmentally. "Always spending everyone else's money on yourself, right Wilfred?" He laughs again, kicking the money around the dirt mindlessly. "You know, we would have made a good politician. Getting paid to spend other people's money is always more fun."

Wilfred's anger mounts, boiling up inside him like a wildfire. A thousand hateful replies race through his mind but all of them feel like lies and taste sour in his mouth.

"Always spending your parent's money on fancy clothes, new cars, houses all over the country, antique books. . ." The clone looks him right in the eyes and shakes his head. Disappointment is the only thing reflected in the duplicant's expression. "You spent all the money on what, vanity? Look at these kids, Wilfred. Look at them!" The clone grabs his chin and forces The Money to look at the starving children. A few of them have begun to pick bloody scraps off of the dead children to eat.

"Think of the lives we could have saved together! We inherited a hundred lifetime's worth of money and then you pissed it all away! How many bottles of scotch would it take to feed this lot? Tell me, Wilfred, tell me!" The clone throws him to the ground and spits on his back, shouting at him and forcing him to watch the starving children eat their own dead.

"I don't know!" The Money finally yells back. Blood dribbles from his finger where he landed on a jagged rock and he can't help but hold it out so his clothes don't get stained. "I never thought of them."

"That's right," the clone mocks. "You only think about yourself." He kicks the stack of bills again and sends it into Wilfred's face.

Filled with rage unlike anything he has ever known, Wilfred pulls the trigger of the Colt Navy until it is empty. The clone takes each hit with a renewed bellow of mocking laughter. "You'll have to do better than that," the duplicate says. "Even the gun in your hands is just another symbol of your vainglory."

"This pistol was my father's!" The Money shouts back. He crawls to his knees and stands, keeping a safe distance between himself and the clone.

"And look how you treat it! You worship that gun; you depend on it like you depend on your wealth." The clone spits into the dirt and turns his back on Wilfred.

"I've taken better care of this pistol than my father ever did!" The Money shouts. In his mind, he knows that he is grasping at straws. The sounds of the starving children behind him fill his mind with guilt.

"You take it out at parties," the clone sneers over his shoulder. "You show it off like a prized mule at a county fair. Tell me, what did our father tell you when he gave it to you?"

The Money hangs his head and he knows that he is defeated. With overwhelming guilt, he drops the pistol and falls back to his knees. "He didn't say anything," he cries. "I stole it from him."

"You rely on physical objects like the gun in your hand and the money in your pocket. What do these things do for you now? Can you feed these children with your dollar bills? Can you feed the least of these with bullet casings?" The clone walks back to Wilfred's crying, huddled form. "It is written, Wilfred Montesquieu, man shall not live on bread alone."

*****

Anders Gronhagen walks onto a grassy field he immediately recognizes. "Stonehenge," he whispers into the breeze. The wind is cool and gentle on his skin. Anders smiles and saunters into the center of the gathered stones. He tilts his head toward the sky and breathes the night air with a smile. The stars shine brightly against the oily black sky and the constellations come alive.

An old man, hobbled and stooped over by his advanced age, walks up to Anders from behind one of the stones and extends his hand. The old man uses a cane to support himself and the act of removing one of his hands from it nearly causes him to fall. Anders catches the man's drooping shoulder as he shakes his hand and helps to upright him.

"Baltasar!" Anders exclaims with joy. "I never thought I would see you again, old friend." Baltasar smiles meekly and returns the handshake with little enthusiasm.

"Anders Gronhagen…" he coughs out the name. "What have you done?" His voice is thick with disappointment and true sorrow.

"I . . . I'm not sure I know what you mean, Baltasar." Anders takes a step back and looks at his old friend, Doctor Kendrick's father.

"Look up at the night sky, Anders," the old man implores. His back is so broken by the passage of time that Baltasar can barely tilt back far enough to see the stars for himself. "Tell me what you see."

Anders studies the constellations and turns slow circles through Stonehenge, tracing the celestial patterns in his mind. "I can see Jupiter, Mars, Mercury; the constellations Aquila, Aquarius, Capricorn… " His voice trails off and he feels at ease among the stars. "I've spent my whole life studying this sky, Baltasar. I can stand here for days and name constellations and stars for you. What is it that you want from me?"

"You are right, old friend, but in your correctness of fact, you have also stated your greatest error." Baltasar spreads his arms as wide as his crippled frame allows, and directs Ander's vision to the rocks of

Stonehenge. "Look at this place. Stonehenge has been a place of pilgrimage for astronomers for years. You, Anders," he points an accusing finger at the younger man's chest. "You visited this site for a decade, every year at the summer solstice without fail."

Growing impatient and increasingly offended, Anders knocks Batlasar's finger away and starts walking out of the stone ring. "I fail to see how my love of astronomy has made me a bad person, Baltasar. As I recall," he sneers with anger in his voice, "it was you who encouraged me to go back to university and get my doctorate! How long have I taught others about astronomy? Is educating another human being not worthy of praise?"

Anders stands in the north-east opening of Stonehenge with his hands on his hips, waiting for a reply. The old man shakes his head in disappointment.

"The celestial bodies arrayed for mankind to observe in the night sky are not meant to be a life's work, Anders," Baltasar says grimly. "You take comfort in your study of the stars and your telescopes. All those years ago, when we met for the first time in Stockholm, why were you at the convention?"

Pacing the grassy area around the stones, Anders searches his memories. "I was a student at the time, going to university there, and the lecture sounded interesting, so I attended."

"You know the real reason why you sat through those lectures, Anders Gronhagen. Why did you sit in the front row, writing down every word I said, and then coming to me after each session for further instruction?" Baltasar raises his cane a few feet from the ground as if prodding the other man to think.

Anders lets out a sigh. "I was searching for something," he admits. "I was lost. Away from home, I didn't know how to make friends. The war was still fresh on everyone's minds, and the world felt doomed. I could accept that most of the people I knew growing up in Sweden were dead before their time." He hangs his head and leans against one of the upright stones to search his innermost thoughts.

"What made you come to my lecture?" Baltasar questions further.

"I needed to know that something… " he struggles for the word, "*larger* existed; larger than me, larger than Sweden and the wars, larger than the world." Anders looks at his old friend and makes no effort to hide his tears. "Astronomy gave me that sense of wonder and blocked out all of the despair."

"You were a wonderful student in the lectures, but you only learned facts," Baltasar states dryly. "Memorizing numbers and names came easily to you, but grasping the larger picture was something you were incapable of conceiving."

"What was I supposed to learn?"

"The real heart of my lecture, and the heart of all astronomy, is not rooted in pure scientific understanding," the old man explains with vigor uncharacteristic of his age. "You take comfort in the study of the stars because you can easily map constellations and remember their names and locations. The true astronomer's comfort comes from viewing the sky and seeing, *truly seeing*, the mastery of creation."

Anders takes a few steps back inside the ring of stone and looks to the sky, trying to decipher their meaning.

"When I look to the stars, I see a wonderful masterpiece of artistry laid out before me. The mysteries of the universe are more complex than any of us can hope to understand, but that is what keeps us in a state of constant awe. The question that all astronomers should ask is how someone skilled enough to create the entire universe has the patience and mercy to know our names." Baltasar waves his cane about the circle wildly, gesturing at everything he sees, and leaning against a stone to keep himself from tumbling over.

"The infinite wonder of creation," Baltasar continues, "is that we can never solve the puzzle. No matter how hard we strive, we cannot know all of the secrets. You busy yourself with the study of facts and numbers and names, but you never take a moment to lean back in your chair and be mesmerized."

Anders turns his eyes heavenward and looks into the vastness of space. After a long silence, he finally admits to himself that his old friend is right. "I guess I let myself become too immersed in the pursuit of knowledge to realize what I was studying."

Baltasar places a weak hand on Ander's shoulder and speaks to him softly. "Remember, a third of the stars will be flung down upon the earth in the end of days, despite whatever knowledge you and the rest of mankind can amass. The real wonder of creation," Baltasar raises his cane and uses it to poke Anders lightly in the stomach, "is the very image of God."

*****

Doctor Kendrick squints to let her eyes adjust to the harsh fluorescent lighting. She in a hospital, one she knows well, and it takes her less than a heartbeat to recognize the moment.

She is standing outside of her office in the first hospital she practiced in after she received her medical degree. Her nameplate on the door reads her birth name, not the alias she hid behind after the accident.

The office door is closed, but Doctor Kendrick knows every word being said behind it by heart. Reaching through the illusionary scene, Lissa opens the door and walks into her old office. A younger version of herself sits behind the desk and idly takes notes on a yellow pad of paper while a teenage girl cries into a pillow.

"Klara, child," the young Lissa tries to soothe, "try to tell me one more time what happened."

The teenage girl is a mess of tears and snotty, heaving sobs. She can barely control her breathing and talking is an entirely unreasonable demand.

"I was a terrible psychologist . . ." The displaced Doctor Kendrick murmurs. She knows exactly what will happen and dreads reliving it again, but there is nowhere else for her to go.

After a long fit of Klara's wild crying, the younger Lissa looks at her watch impatiently and calls for a nurse to bring a sedative into the room. When the teenage girl sees the syringe in the nurse's hand, she jolts her body upright and suddenly calms. "She was trying to avoid the drugs, you stupid bitch," Doctor Kendrick chastises her young self. "Why couldn't you see that? Klara wasn't actually calming down."

Klara, a sixteen-year-old girl, was found by the police during a manhunt. The police task force was being used to hunt down an international criminal suspected of illegal weapons trafficking. Instead of guns and military paraphernalia, the police found Klara. She was naked, covered in bruises, and chained to the bottom of a boat used to ferry girls in the sex trade to and from the Soviet-controlled Baltic ports and the free territories of northern Europe.

Doctor Kendrick was assigned as Klara's psychological examiner before the teenager would be allowed to testify in court against the man who kidnapped her. To the young psychologist right out of medical school, the case was boring and Lissa didn't expect to have Klara as a patient for very long. The state would probably claim the battered girl and have her committed to a sanitarium after the trial, she thought.

The younger Lissa stands and walks to the girl, sitting on the couch next to her. She places a gentle arm around Klara, patting the young girl on the back. "That's enough for today's session," she says quietly. The distraught girl nods her head and runs for the door, nearly tripping over the psychologist in the process.

The displaced Doctor Kendrick sucks in her breath and tries to move out of the way but the running teenager hurries through her incorporeal body. A sensation of dizziness accompanies the motion and makes Lissa tumble to the side. The girl darts into the hallway and a shriek of screams echoes through the hospital.

Doctor Kendrick knows why Klara is screaming without walking back into the corridor. She watches as the younger version of herself chases after Klara. The young girl is standing in the hallway, holding a small paring knife, and ripping her left wrist open.

Blood sprays against the white walls of the hospital and nurses scramble to hold the girl. Klara swings the small blade around in an arc before her, keeping the nurses and Doctor Kendrick at bay. The girl snarls, leaning against the wall for support, and thrashes her shredded arm. Thick droplets of blood rain from her skin to stain the nurses' uniforms.

Klara lets loose a howl of deranged anger and sinks the knife into her stomach. Her eyes bore into the young Doctor Kendrick and the girl sneers, dropping to the ground where she is instantly swarmed by the nurses and strapped to a stretcher. The girl is taken to the emergency room and ultimately saved, but Doctor Kendrick knows that she will not live until the trial.

The illusionary scene fades away like mist and is replaced by another moment, days after Klara attempted to kill herself. Doctor Kendrick stands in the back of a plain church building as Klara's family members file by to touch the closed casket. Her younger self is not present, Lissa knows, and that fact brings her shame.

A voice from behind her startles the woman. She turns and sees Pastor Santiago walking slowly towards her with his head reverently bowed. "Lissa Kendricksson," he calls to her softly. "What have you done?"

"You think I killed Klara?" She exclaims defensively. "I would never do such a terrible thing."

Pastor Santiago stands before her in his customary robe and looks up into her eyes. "Whatever role you might have played in the untimely suicide of that young woman has nothing to do with the reason you stand in this church right now."

Lissa turns away momentarily, pondering the words but not understanding. Whirling back on the pastor, she accuses him. "You brought me here to torment me with my worst memories?" she yells into his face.

"When Klara killed herself, you allowed your own spirit to die, Lissa Kendricksson." Pastor Santiago stands like a statue, betraying no emotion on his face and never looking away.

"What do you mean?" Lissa asks tentatively. She can sense his answer coming and does not want to face it.

"When was the last time you regularly attended church, Lissa?" Pastor asks. "When was the last time you prayed?"

"I won't let you torture me like this," she barks. "I went to church every Sunday in medical school, praying that the patients I saw would heal and get better. Klara was one of my first cases . . ." Her voice trails off and Lissa's mind is overrun by images of Klara's suicide.

Three days after she stabbed herself in the hospital hallway, the traumatized teenager was brought back to her to receive electric shock treatment. That night, locked in her room at the hospital, Klara managed to unscrew a metal table leg. The nurses at their station couldn't hear the young girl striking herself in the throat with the makeshift club over and over. The coroner said that for a woman her size, it must have taken her hours to kill herself.

"You never forgave yourself for Klara," Pastor Santiago says quietly. His empathetic eyes turn toward the casket at the front of the church. The man lifts a robed arm up and points, ushering Doctor

Kendrick to say her last goodbyes. "Do not let her death lead to the annihilation of your soul, Lissa."

"I was ridiculed in the press for her treatment. My own friends said that I killed her. The court case fell apart with her suicide and the man who tortured her walked free . . ." A lump forms in her throat and warm tears flow freely down her face, dripping onto the soft red carpet. She walks slowly to the casket, watching the family members file past her. Klara's parents are inconsolable. They weep openly, letting their sorrow take the form of loud, acrimonious wails.

A single candle is lit atop the wooden casket and it flickers when Lissa approaches. One of Klara's relatives stands next to Lissa at the front of the church and shivers. The man looks over his shoulder and seems confused, rubbing his arms and neck as though they were suddenly cold. "I am a ghost . . ." Lissa utters. Fear grips her body and claws for space at the back of her mind. "No," she cries tenderly. "Fletcher . . ."

*****

I walk through the large door underneath the woodland fortress and expect some sort of hellish nightmare to strike me down. The area beyond is blank, filled with nothing but dark space that has not been formed.

"Hello?" I say, turning around and witnessing the vastness of empty space surrounding me. "Hello? Is anyone there?"

"Your friends have gone to their judgments, Fletcher Lee." A familiar, hissing voice fills the darkness and I know that it is the featureless man.

"They haven't done anything wrong," I reply. "They only wanted to help me." The featureless man materializes in front of me, standing against the blackness of empty space. His wrinkled head juts forward from his shoulders like a person straining to see something far in the distance.

My first thought is to cut the demon down where he stands. The featureless man's head hovers so close to my face that it wouldn't be difficult. I pull the dagger from my belt silently and move it into position under the scaly, pale chin.

Memories of cutting through scores of the demons in the bizarre house at the end of my street make me think twice. I bring the dagger down another inch, still gripping it tightly, and the featureless man cocks his head. He reminds me of my dog, turning her head whenever someone bounced a tennis ball, and I have to choke back a laugh. My mind wanders to the mill and I can feel the heat of the fire warming my body. The weight of my past bores into my consciousness and makes me sick to my stomach.

I drop the dagger as I consider what I did to my own mother's animated corpse. The metal blade falls from my hand, pulled by gravity into the silent darkness, and quickly fades from my view.

The demon jerks away from me as though something struck it violently in the head. Spidery fingers clutch at the side of the blank face and the demon hisses again. The creature's voice is full of hatred and evil, but I can sense an underlying layer of fear beneath all of the contempt as he shrieks.

"I am done with you, demon," I state flatly with a tone bolstered by confidence. The featureless man vanishes before me in a small puff of acrid smoke and in his place, a man clothed with fire stands.

The fiery being smiles and I know that I am safe. Deep within the recesses of my mind I feel a wave of comfort. The memories of my actions, the rush of victory I felt after murdering a kid in the street, my most heinous moments are nothing but the wisps of hazy inklings. "I have been searching for you, Fletcher Lee," the man says with a voice resounding like thunder. It is loud, filling my consciousness with its presence, but it doesn't hurt my ears. The voice is everywhere at once, surrounding me and echoing off of things I cannot see.

"Why am I here?" I want to know. The man's fire is so bright that it should have blinded me, but somehow I am able to look upon his visage without strain.

"I have revealed myself to you, Fletcher, and that is something you must never take lightly." The flames grow higher and higher as the man speaks, but they don't burn my flesh or singe my hairs. The fire dances and rolls, casting a vibrant glow against the utter darkness.

"Are you the Son of the Morning?" I ask slowly, entranced by the moving flames. "Is this Hell?"

"No, Fletcher Lee, you are not in Hell." Relief hits me like a wave of renewal cleansing the impurities from my psyche. "I am not the Bringer of the Dawn, but you will meet him again before your time is done. The Great Deceiver lurks in every shadow, waiting to devour. Stand tall, Fletcher, for your trials have served as a window for others to view redemption."

"I . . ." My mind swirls, thinking of Doctor Kendrick and the other two men who came through the portal to save me. "I don't think I understand."

The flaming man chuckles softly, sending spurts of fire leaping into the darkness. "You will never understand your personal torments, just as you will never be able to comprehend the evil that tears your world asunder. What matters is that you stand tall, unashamed, and never falter."

I nod, trying to fathom everything in light of what has happened, but cannot truly understand. "Am I dead?" I wonder aloud. I don't know how long I have been away from my dad, if he is still alive, or if the world even exists as I once knew it.

"I cannot answer that, my son. It is not the place of mankind to know the times appointed for such souls to be recalled to their rightful stations in the book of life. You will return to the material plane, but you may die within moments. Or you may live so long that Methuselah looks upon you with envy. I cannot say."

"That isn't particularly comforting," I respond.

The fiery man laughs again, sending his booming voice to fill the void that encompasses the two of us. "Life is never comforting, Fletcher, but trust me, knowing the exact moment you will die is far more troubling."

"I guess," I say, trying to find the mirth in such a dark topic. "Martha, the dwarf witch, she told me something. I am supposed to make arrows for the Son of the Morning. What does it mean?" I ask.

Wednesday, November 17th, 1976

"You're leaving already?" Pastor Santiago asks, seated behind his cluttered desk.

"I must," Lissa replies. She runs a nervous hand through her hair and struggles to meet Santiago's gaze. Being in the dark and musty office makes the hair on the back of her neck stand on end. Meager rays of sunlight filter through the dusty window to illuminate the side of Santiago's robes.

Lissa takes *The Keys of Solomon* out of her briefcase and slides it across the table. "I'm afraid I never got a chance to read this," she whispers with more than a hint of regret. "Has there been any word from Montesquieu?" She tentatively asks, fearing the answer.

Pastor Santiago shakes his head. "He cannot die in Gehenna, but I am worried that he may be trapped." Santiago lets out a long sigh leans back in his chair.

"I saw Anders last night before I left the hospital," Doctor Kendrick says as she stands from her chair. "He isn't doing well..."

"He is an old man," Santiago replies, trying to comfort her. "Perhaps it is his time."

A heavy silence fills the air between them and Doctor Kendrick cannot shake the feeling that returning to Sweden is a mistake.

"Have you spoken with Fletcher?" Lissa finally breaks the silence.

Santiago's lips twitch into a temporary smile at the mention of the boy's name. "I convinced Rich to let me enroll Fletcher in one of our Bible camps. With a little luck, perhaps we can begin to reintroduce Fletcher to the world."

Lissa reaches out and shakes Santiago's hand firmly. "With everything that Fletcher has been through, he might never be able to fully come to terms with his past."

"Even from birth, that boy has had an unfortunate life." Santiago ushers the doctor out of the office with a wave of his hand.

Doctor Kendrick walks out of the church with a head full of doubts. "I don't recall Pastor Santiago being aware of Fletcher's birth story..." Lissa brushes the notion from her mind and drives out of the parking lot, heading in the direction of the airport.

*****

Pastor Santiago watches Lissa's departure from one of the stained glass windows of the church.

"You're sure he will be at the camp?" A voice from the shadows questions.

"Yes, my lord," Santiago snaps. "This is the third time I have handed him over to you. I do not know if you will get a fourth chance."

Monday, November 22<sup>nd</sup>, 1976

I sit in the back of a yellow bus filled with kids. A huge smile is plastered to my face. I'm not going to school, despite my begging, but my dad is sending me to a religious camp that sounds like a lot of fun. Camp Faithful; I like that name. I asked if Doctor Kendrick was going to be at the camp, but my dad said that she had moved back to her hometown in Sweden. I won't get to see her again.

"My trials are a window for others to view redemption..." I whisper. The simple sentence brings me comfort. I know beyond a doubt that I have been saved. In the two days since my return to the world, everything has been perfect. My dad found a real job teaching at a high school and I was finally able to convince him to sell the orange Javelin.

"My trials are a window for others to view redemption," I repeat, staring at the soft leather cover of my Bible. The book bounces on my lap as the bus takes a few potholes at full speed.

"What?" the cute girl across the aisle asks me. She sits with her legs wedged up against the top of the seat in front of her and talks to another camper.

"Oh, nothing," I tell her, looking out the window. I remember scaring the kids in school with the things I said, so I decided that being the 'quiet kid' is the best way to ease myself back into normal society.

The bus hits another pothole in the bumpy road and some of the kids sitting at the front cheer. They clap with every jolt and jump of the bus. Pastor Santiago stands up at the head of the bus, leaning closely over the driver, and watches the road as we motor along. A girl up front yells that she has to go to the bathroom, but I can tell that she is just joking to make the boys laugh.

We hit another pothole in the road and this time, when the bus reconnects with the pavement, it leans heavily to the right and I can see the driver losing control. The boy in front of me turns around in a panic and for an instant his eyes, mouth, and nose vanish into a pile of wrinkled skin.

"No!" I scream, fighting the urge to hit the boy in the face. My fist clenches and I remember the feel of blood staining my fingers. *The featureless man is gone,* I remind myself. *I will make arrows for the Son of the Morning*, I recite, trying to find comfort in the mantra.

The bus careens through the concrete barrier in the center of the road and rolls onto its side with a deafening crash.

"Just keep looking at me…" I hear from somewhere far away.

An impact shakes the bus violently, but so far, I am not hurt. I open my eyes just enough to peek through the glass of the emergency exit door one seat behind me. Children cry and scream, but there aren't enough voices. There were so many of us going to camp, there should be more screams. Pastor Santiago tries to yell something from the front of the bus but is overcome by coughing and spitting.

A car comes hurtling into view, swerving all over the road. I brace myself against the itchy bus seat but in the back of my mind, I know that it is not enough. The car is moving too quickly and heading right for the back of the bus.

"I will make arrows!" I shout defiantly. The impact steals all of the air from my lungs and blackens my vision. I try to recall an image of the fiery man in mind to bring me some shred of reassurance but that moment feels like it happens centuries ago. For a heartbeat, everything is silent.

In the quiet solitude of impending oblivion, I am thankful that I do not know when I will die.

Acknowledgment:

Special thanks to everyone who has helped in the creation of not only this novel, but all of my works. Not enough thanks can be heaped upon the shoulders of those who bring my work to life.

About the author:

Stuart Thaman is the author of several novels, including Vatican Massacre, a National Novel Writing Month Winner and an Amazon.com best seller, as well as The Goblin Wars fantasy series.

Stuart graduated from Hillsdale College with degrees in German and Politics. He currently lives in Cincinnati, Ohio, and teaches German and philosophy for the Diocese of Covington. When not writing, Stuart enjoys spending time outdoors and going to metal concerts. Visit Thaman on Facebook and Goodreads, and email him at stuartthaman@gmail.com